PO-2

THE PROOF
OF THE HONEY

Salwa Al Neimi

THE PROOF
OF THE HONEY

Translated by Carol Perkins

Europa
editions

5 - 09
15 -

Europa Editions
116 East 16th Street
New York, N.Y. 10003
www.europaeditions.com
info@europaeditions.com

Library of Congress Cataloging in Publication Data is available
ISBN 978-1-933372-68-6

Al Neimi, Salwa
The Proof of the Honey

Book design by Emanuele Ragnisco
www.mekkanografici.com
Cover photo © Marie Accomiato

Prepress by Plan.ed – Rome

Printed in Canada

CONTENTS

First Gate
ON MARRIAGES OF PLEASURE AND BOOKS OF EROTICA - 11

Second Gate
ON THE THINKER AND PERSONAL HISTORY - 27

Third Gate
SEX AND THE (ARAB) CITY - 39

Fourth Gate
ON WATER - 47

Fifth Gate
ON STORIES - 53

Sixth Gate
ON THE MASSEUSE AND HER ADULTEROUS HUSBAND - 73

Seventh Gate
ON THE ECSTASIES OF THE BODY - 89

Eighth Gate
ON ARAB DISSIMULATION - 99

Ninth Gate
ON LINGUISTICS - 107

Tenth Gate
ON UPBRINGING AND EDUCATION - 115

Eleventh Gate
ON RUSES - 133

ABOUT THE AUTHOR - 143

The desired face is neither a memory nor a dream.
It combines the two and goes beyond them.
The desired face prolongs the moment of desire indefinitely.
—UNSI AL HAJJ

Body, remember not only how much you were loved,
not only the beds you lay on, but also those desires glowing
openly in eyes that looked at you,
trembling for you in voices—
only some chance obstacle frustrated them.
Now that it's all finally in the past,
it seems almost as if you gave yourself
to those desires, too—how they glowed,
remember, in the eyes that looked at you, remember, body,
how they trembled for you in those voices.
—CAVAFY[1]

I will come to her bare headed, bare footed.
—SALIM RIZQALLAH

Tomorrow, the day after, or years later, he'll give voice
to the strong lines that had their beginning here.
—CAVAFY[2]

[1] Cavafy, C. P., *Collected Poems*. Translated by Edmund Keeley and Philip Sherrard, edited by George Savidis. London, Chatto and Windus, 1994 (p. 59).
[2] Idem (p. 81).

First Gate

ON MARRIAGES OF PLEASURE
AND BOOKS OF EROTICA

Some people conjure spirits. I conjure bodies. I have no knowledge of my soul or of the souls of others. I know only my body and theirs.

And I content myself with that.

I conjure them and I see myself with them once again—ephemeral travelers in an ephemeral body; they were never more than that. The rules had been laid down. What, men as mere objects? And why not?

As lovers? What a big word. I can never bring myself to use it, even to myself. The Thinker uttered it, once, and I was shocked. *Lover?* I don't have lovers. There must be another word, of course, but I haven't bothered looking for it. One day, as I was telling him about a girlfriend of mine who'd met him at a party, he asked me lightly, "Does she know I'm your lover?" Nobody knew about him and it wasn't the question that offended me. It was the word. Lover!

The Thinker, my lover? The idea had never occurred to me. Could I be the mistress of a man from whom I ask only one thing: that he hold me in his arms in a closed room? Could I be the mistress of a man from whom I ask only stolen hours?

I didn't analyze the matter further because at that juncture, as was his habit, the Thinker said, "I have an idea." He approached the bed. I lay on my stomach, my back arched, my weight resting on my forearms. He was behind me and I couldn't see him. He caressed me, tracing the curves of my body from my shoulders to my thighs, stopping at my buttocks. He pulled me towards him. I pressed against him more tightly to fill myself with him. I buried my face in the pillow to stifle the gasps of pleasure that accompanied our movements and our words. I knew that in coition "the more shameless it is the better," but still, I tried to stifle my moans.

He again pulled me to him, into that particular position that I love best, that he loves best.

In that position, our points of view converge despite the difference in our respective angles. What matters is the point of convergence.

I silenced my noises. I forgot my girlfriends. I dissolve exegesis and theory into the experimental fusion of bodies.

Lovers? The Thinker undoubtedly had legitimate reasons for using the word. But I couldn't! I was coming from a planet with a different language—a planet with a woman's language, one that I had been obliged to invent. Usually, I resort to the dictionaries, but they don't always give me what I want. Their language and their concepts only hinder me. Their definition of the word "lover" is too broad to be applied to the men I've known.

Even the Thinker?

Lovers?

In the beginning is the encounter. First, a certain flash of eyes, then my reply, categorical. I feel my answer rising in the first instant, even before the suitor presents letters of accreditation for his lust. All that matters is my own desire, my rare desire.

The Yes or the No comes of its own volition after a single glance. The decision is made. All the rules are erased. I listen only to my own voice. The voice of my desire, my rare desire.

My sense of morality bears no relation to the values of the world that surrounds me, values I rejected long ago. This moral sense guides my actions and measures them according to principles I alone have determined. My only concern is the effect of my actions on my life—my face after love, the gleam in my eyes, the gathering together of my scattered parts, the words that burn in my breast and the stories they ignite.

Orandum est, ut sit mens sana in corpore sano. One must pray to obtain a sound mind in a sound body. Health, through sex. Even before finding the echo of my own thoughts in the Arab erotic literature that is so dear to me, I had understood.

The Traveler said: You have known no man but your husband.

He said: You refuse every man who desires you because your principles lead you to fear society and the judgment of men.

He said: This is what remains of your old-fashioned upbringing; you are paralyzed, curbed, fettered, you understood "yes" as resignation and nothing more.

He said: You are afraid your radiance will fade in the eyes of any man whose advances you accept.

He said: You have no confidence in your body and you do not dare to stand naked before a man.

He said: You refuse to follow the example of your girlfriend, the one who says yes to all men. You consider her easy.

I said: "Maybe," aware that I was light years away from all that.

I said: "Maybe," so that I wouldn't have to tell him that my physical rejection of him didn't mean my absolute rejection of all men.

I said: "Maybe," and let him believe that I accepted his interpretations, and I was satisfied with the success of that subtle ploy I often use.

Does the fact that I reject one man mean I reject them all? Does my saying no to one man's desire mean that I'm saying no to all men? It's a dominant male interpretation, which suits everybody, most of all me.

I used to say "maybe" because I didn't want to explain. What kind of explanation could I have given? That I accept no authority outside my own will: neither their principles, nor their values, nor their ethics? Neither society, nor religion, nor tradition? Neither the fear of others' tongues, nor the terror of punishment, nor the flames of hell?

I am polygamous by nature, I know it. Like almost all women. We are taught the opposite, but I know that my nature is polygamous. Though that is not exactly the right term. I ought to say "polyamourous" or at least "polyandrous."

Years ago I heard Alberto Moravia speaking about "natural promiscuity" in women and his words fell on my ears like a revelation. He put into words things I felt and that were part of my life. Afterwards, I read the same phrase from the pen of a contemporary French philosopher theorizing about pleasure and applying the idea of promiscuity to all humans, male and female. I happily read and reread his book, though I wasn't in need of him—my life was nothing if not a demonstration of his ideas.

Was Moravia before or after the Thinker? I can no longer recall.

Was the French philosopher before or after the Thinker? I can no longer recall.

All I know is that I encountered the Thinker at the height of my readings of the classics of erotic literature. I started amusing myself by transposing everything that happened between us into the ancient texts. I would read these to him, going to great lengths in their deconstruction. He knew only one of them—*The Book of Voluptuousness: By Which the Old Man Returns to His Youth.*

I had read it in secret at the start of my adolescence. A school companion lent it to me. She was a few years older than the rest of us; she used lipstick and mascara. Mysterious stories circulated about her, though only snippets were told in front of us younger students—of the traces of blows on her body, of her family who wanted to marry her off against her will, of her constant assertion that she would rub the family's name in the dirt to get back at them, of the boys waiting boldly for her at the school gate.

I can no longer recall when I saw her with this book of hers or how she came to lend it to me, making me swear as she did so that no one else should see it. I remember my initial shock, and my fear that someone would catch me with it. No one monitored what I read or restricted my freedom, but I felt intuitively that I was committing an act that I had to hide from others. The speed with which I read it reflected my apprehension. All I remember is my longing to discover, and the fear of the panorama that was opening up before me. My eyes were glued to the pages and my heart raced. I hid it among my school books and returned it to its owner the following day. She shot me a look of expectant curiosity. I placed it in her hands and gave nothing away. Disappointed by my silence, she took it and hid it in her bag, turning her back on me.

I was young but the foundations of my secret worlds had already been laid. From early on I possessed a talent for dissembling and I used it to create a protective barrier separating my freedom from the world's hypocrisy.

A few years later, my adventures provided ample occasion for me to put the teachings of my Arab masters to the test. I recognized "the benefits of the sexual act" for the body, mind, and spirit—namely, that "It calms anger and brings joy to the soul of those whose natures are ardent. It is also a sure treatment for the darkening of the sight, for the circulation, for heaviness of the head, and for pains in the sides such as blind the heart and close the gates of thought."

I also learnt of the harm I would suffer if I abstained. According to Muhammad ibn Zakariya:

Whoever abandons coition for long periods suffers the weakening of his organs; his blood circulates poorly, and his member will be weakened. I have observed those who abandon intercourse in order to live a chaste life: their bodies turned cold and their movements awkward, and a causeless dejection fell upon them. The diseases associated with melancholia were common among them, and they were listless, and had difficulty digesting their food.

Psychological and physical diseases? Madness, dejection, and melancholia all at once? God protect us and let us not refuse sex!

Said Ibn al-Azraq: "Every desire to which a man surrenders himself hardens his heart, except for coition." I am determined to keep my heart tender.

When it came to the question of coition, theory was my disguise. I quoted from books or gave examples from other people's lives. But my own parallel life was hidden in a lamp that I rubbed only when I was alone, when I would release the genie of memory.

Then along came the Thinker and I told him, "Yes."

At first I didn't tell anyone about my epistemological passion. Those books were my secret, one that I shared with nobody. The Thinker came along and I said "Yes." The Thinker came along and I opened the door. In the hollow of our bed, I told him about my secret readings. The two secrets—him and my readings—mingled and merged into a single torrent.

In those days it was enough for me to find pleasure in my books, as I read them again with him. I would commit the name of each position to memory and describe them to him. The names—usually comic—became a secret code with which we communicated with one other in seeming innocence, sprinkling our conversation with them in the presence of others and skillfully passing them back and forth to one another in every context. It wasn't always easy: how could one place terms such as "the funnel," "the battering ram," "the bellows," "the twister," and "threading the beads" in the midst of meaningful sentences? The ignorance of others merely enhanced our pleasure in the game that we played so shamelessly.

I was confident that no one who was not an expert in the Books of erotica—who had not, like me, read them over and over again—would give any thought to such words, and such experts were rare, even among persons of culture versed in the canon. I confirmed this through the use of amusing practical experiments.

Thanks to the Thinker I grasped the value of my secret books. I went from Ahmad ibn Yusuf al-Tifashi to Ali ibn Nasr, from al-Samaw'al ibn Yahya to Nasr al-Din al-Tusi, Muhammad al-Nafzawi, and Ahmad ibn Sulayman, to Ali al-Katibi al-Qazwini, al-Suyuti, and al-Tijani as if from the company of one friend to that of another. I would read them and then reread them, sampling their texts, translating my life into their words, and retaining these as a secret language that I dared divulge to no one but the Thinker.

Why this common ground between the Thinker and my secret books?

With him I progressed to a stage of sexual awareness that was inseparable from my readings. My gestures gave life to words, which in turn ordered my gestures, and from this exchange flew hissing sparks. I played at transforming what I experienced with him into passages from the books. I would share these with him on the spot and he would look at me in astonishment and say, "These things are a hidden treasure known only to the few. They must be written about and made known."

The Thinker was my secret and the books were a part of that secret.

The freedom of the ancients would mock me. They employed an array of words that I didn't dare to use myself, either in speech or in writing; a language of arousal that made me wet whenever I read even a line. No other language could excite me that way. Arabic, for me, is the language of sex. No foreign language can match it at the moment of passion, even with those who don't speak it—in such moments, there is no need for translation, naturally.

The forbidden words brought to life a history of sexual repression and of the resistance to that repression. Ironically, I never used such words myself, even in my innermost thoughts—they were only to be read, never spoken or written. Even today, I find it difficult to use any of the rawest of these words in my ordinary speech. I avoid them. I can copy them and I can quote them with all the innocence of a child, but using them to speak of myself and my own experiences is another matter.

These texts are a part of my universe. They are a part of my imagination. These texts are a part of my sex life—before the Thinker, and with him, and after him. In this filigree of intertwined experience, it is impossible to unpick the smallest thread. The interconnectedness is organic. Organic, indeed—what other word can I use?

At first, I didn't want this filigree to be pulled apart. I didn't want to take off the veil, to proclaim it. I never dared speak of it.

Is the scandal in the act or in the proclamation of the act? I astonished myself with my own question—my teachers among the ancients were far beyond it. "Scandal," did I say? What is scandalous about it?

Was it my being a woman that made my secret readings so explosive?

Was making a secret of it part of my emasculated

upbringing? Why was it possible for me to take pride in my reading of Western and Eastern pornography while hiding the fact that I was reading al-Tifashi? How could I proclaim my passion for Georges Bataille, Henry Miller, the Marquis de Sade, Casanova, and the Kama Sutra and make no mention of al-Suyuti and al-Nafzawi? Anyway, that's past history, and my hidden readings have now become fashionable—everyone talks about them, not least myself. My old secret has been told and exposed to the light.

Told, exposed to the light, and become "like the thyme-seller's wink"—seen by one and all.

With the passing of the years, I have become less uptight and so has everyone else. Little by little, pleasantries, laughter, and comments have come. I have begun making my literary tastes public, all the more since the days of the Thinker. The books I read have become a topic of conversation at the library. Some of my colleagues regard these books as a game, others consider them a form of deviancy, and some picture the stories to themselves, magnifying them and swapping them with each other in whispers.

My secret vices are no longer secret and I no longer have to be clandestine or to hide the covers of the books. I revel in every new erotic volume to arrive on our shelves, proclaiming my joy to the world. Indeed, there are now among my colleagues those who hurry to bring the good tidings to my attention whenever they happen across a book of which I was unaware. Over time, books of erotica have become a harmless fantasy. I am no different from my colleague who searches for books on cooking, or the woman who works on old maps. Respectable pastimes, all.

*

Early on, I knew my path. I knew the game I would play. That game amused me, was part of my secret life. Nobody could claim to be the overseer of my nights; nobody could claim to be the marshal of my liberties. My life was my own. My secrets, too.

Early on I knew my path and my game was simple: I would never hide what I thought, however much it might shock others. I would hide only my actions. This in itself was dangerous enough in an environment where dissimulation and submission reigned.

When I announced one day in front of my male and female colleagues gathered around the lunch table that monogamy was contrary to nature, that fidelity was merely an illusion, that sexual desire needed freedom in order to flourish, and so on, they looked at me with mistrust and suspicion before embarking on a heated discussion in which I took no part. My game consists of throwing out words and observing their effect.

From Marguerite Duras I learned to conceal from my lovers the love I felt for my husband. And to conceal from my husband the love I felt for my lovers: that I learned from all women.

I learned to be the sole guardian of my nights. My secret could never be known because I told it to no one. Is a secret that is shared by two people no longer a secret? No. Any secret that is shared is not a secret.

My recurring nightmare took the form of one unchanging scenario: there was a corpse hidden somewhere and I was the murderer. I had hidden the corpse carefully and I lived in terror of its being discovered. I would scheme in vain to prevent the others from seeing it, but sooner or later they would. The nightmare was set in those moments that preceded the discovery of my crime, of the corpse, of all my hidden secrets. I would open my eyes in the darkness, trembling with terror. "The skeleton's in the closet," as the proverb says. Everything was clear; I didn't need an expert to interpret these dreams.

I lost my memory of things at will: a useful trick for living in this society. I would erase memories or keep them at will—over long years I practiced this art until I was so supple at it that it required no thought.

I was my own role model. I had no need of worldly or heavenly guidance. I had no need of a *fatwa* that would allow me to cling to my men in the fever hours. Mr. Quick loved to tell a certain story. Once upon a time he had a colleague, a woman journalist. They were on assignment together and she knocked on the door of his hotel room one night, well after midnight, to ask him to be one of the witnesses to a rapidly arranged wedding. The African who had caught her fancy, and whose fancy she had caught, had refused to sleep with her in a state of sin; he needed two witnesses for his one-night marriage. Mr. Quick told the story to anyone who'd listen, and everyone, gloating and sneering, passed it on as if they, too, had been there. I remember I told it to the Thinker and we amused ourselves running through names in search of anyone we knew who could serve as our own witness.

Such a marriage is called a "marriage of pleasure." It is permitted to Shiites, and only to Shiites. Could I consider every man I'd known (in the Biblical sense) "a husband of pleasure"?

A marriage of pleasure? The basic contradiction

between the two nouns is evident. The first makes a slave
of the spirit. The second frees it.

Perhaps the virtue in a marriage of pleasure is that it
lasts only as long as the pleasure lasts. Its other virtue lies
in the fact that the pleasure to be found in it is legal, licit,
halal. Without the "for all eternity" part, marriage isn't
quite so burdensome—is it not so?

The "marriage of pleasure" is for Shiites only. That
doesn't concern me in the least. I do not recognize com-
munalism or religious divisions. In any case, I cannot consider my passing men to be "husbands of pleasure"
because I have yet to fulfill the rules of religious law, which
states:

> The marriage of foreshortened term, like that which is
> permanent, requires a contract that includes positive
> oral response and acceptance, the inward consent of
> the two parties being insufficient. It follows that the
> contract of a marriage of pleasure is, unambiguously, a
> legal contract, with all the latter's conditions. It is
> reported on the authority of Aban ibn Taghlib that he
> said to Abu 'Abd al-Rahman: "How should a man
> make a contract with a woman if he finds himself alone
> with her?" And he replied: "You say, I marry you for
> pleasure according to God's Book and the practice of
> His prophet, without your acquiring the right to inher-
> it or to pass on by inheritance, for so and so many days.
> If she replies in the positive then she has consented
> and thus become your wife, and the priority of your
> claim to her over that of all other people is estab-
> lished."

I wonder where the African came up with the clause about the two witnesses. I can't find a trace of it in the books of Muslim jurisprudence. Indeed, that never concerned me; in my secret rites, I made do with the announcement of desire through the body. After all that I'd read and studied and learned and been taught, nothing remained in my head but the word "desire," and the pleasure of its satisfaction.

Second Gate

ON THE THINKER AND PERSONAL HISTORY

The Thinker is a tale on his own.

My life is divided into two halves—Before the Thinker and After the Thinker. I would come to him completely wet. It was enough for me to think of him and I would be ready for love.

The Thinker would say: "You're always aroused. I've never seen you when you weren't ready for love." I'd smile, thinking it unnecessary to explain that he was the reason for my readiness. I would just throw myself on him and my analysis would be confirmed.

Once, on the metro, I was deep in thought, reliving an encounter with him, when I noticed that the man sitting opposite was staring at me. He was looking at me as though he were reading my thoughts. As though he were watching a pornographic film. Was it not the Thinker himself, one day when we were seated in a café and I could hardly contain my lust for him, who said, "I've never before known a woman whose face proclaimed her 'erection.'"

I would come to him wet and *he* would slip his finger between my legs, looking for "the honey," as he used to call it, tasting it and kissing me and pushing his tongue deep into my mouth. "Clearly, you follow the Prophet's commandments," I'd say, "and take him as your model, for did he not say, 'Let not one of you fall upon your folk as a beast does, but let there be between you a messenger—the kiss, and conversation.' And A'isha, the Prophet's favorite wife, said, 'the messenger of God, when he kissed one among us, would suck on her tongue.'"

How could I refute such a heritage? How could I not remind the Thinker of it? He had no need of anyone to remind him of his heritage. In such things he was a Muslim par excellence, as was I.

I would go to him in the morning before work. I would run up the steps. A light ring on the bell and he would open the door immediately, as though he had been waiting for me behind it, half asleep. I would throw off my clothes and slip into the bed. I would cling to him and start sniffing him. He would raise the cover and his hand would caress me, slowly. Grave and happy, he would taste my honey. I would investigate every place on his body with my lips. My eyes were open, and likewise my body. Between my greedy haste and his appreciative deliberation we found our rhythm. Time passed, we remained together. Beneath him, above him, to the side of him, flat on my belly, or on my knees; between each position and the next, he would repeat his pet phrase: "I have an idea." He was never short on ideas. As for me, I adore philosophy, the world of ideas. I named him "The Thinker."

The Thinker is a tale on his own. My life is divided into two halves—yes, BT and AT. Before him was my prehistoric age.

Which does not mean that I was a virgin either in spirit or in body. I was neither the one nor the other. I was not like Eve, "who asked Adam the first time he slept with her, 'What is this?' and he said, 'They call it fucking,' to which she replied, 'Fuck me again, for it is good.'"

I, for all my practical experience and my secret and public readings, was only dimly aware of what pleasure was. It
was like a blurry picture. The Thinker came, and contours
appeared. The lines and the colors became clear, the light-
ing focused. I no longer acted my part. I became myself.

BT, was that not my Prehistoric Age?

I would meet men. I would fancy them, and they would
fancy me. I knew what I wanted from them and I didn't
care what they wanted from me. Pages covered with words
written on top of one another, accumulating, not a single
one ever erased. In the end, what was spread out before
me was a spoiled draft whose symbols no one could make
sense of, not even myself—pages written in a secret code.
The Thinker came to shine a light on the code and make
sense of the symbols. He did not sweep the past aside but
bestowed upon me a key with which to read the
palimpsest of my life.

AT was the Age of the Sexual Renaissance, my own personal renaissance, and everything that I lived thereafter,
with other men, was colored by my time with him.

This has nothing to do with the satisfaction of appetite.

Before him I was complete unto myself, replete,
quenched—and it showed. The Traveler had seen it.
When a friend of mine complained that a lesbian had
tried to seduce her, I replied: "No lesbians ever tried to
seduce me."

The Traveler interrupted: "You exude the scent of men,
how do you expect a woman to want to seduce you . . ."

The Thinker used to tell me, "So far you've been used
to filling up on fast food. You'll know another kind of
nourishment with me." Was he right?

Perhaps.

He used to tell me, "There are two kinds of women—
lettuce women, and women of embers." "What am I?" I'd
ask slyly. He wouldn't answer but would pull me to his
chest and I'd throw myself on him and kiss his eyes and his
lips and taste his saliva, and he'd run his hand over my
belly and I'd open my legs and he'd enter me deeply burning in consort with me. I wanted to ask: And men? How
many types of men are there?

But my pleasure made me forget all questions.

We had one rhythm from the beginning. We didn't
need to practice, or tune our instruments. He would be
astonished and proclaim his astonishment. I wouldn't have
time to share in his proclamations. My time was dedicated
wholly to pleasure. I would fall silent. I would cling to his
body and bury my face beneath his armpit and breathe his
smell deeply into my chest.

"The benefits of intercourse are in the first place the
satisfaction of lust, in the second the enjoyment of pleasure, and in the third healing."

Behind the closed door he'd give me a farewell
embrace. We never could leave one another without ado.
He'd kiss me and kiss me again. I couldn't pull myself
away. I'd kneel down in front of him and bend over and
rub my face against him and want it to fill my mouth,
almost choking with longing. It would grow as I sucked
greedily down to the last drop and then raise my eyes to
watch his face, tense with pleasure. His head was thrown
back, his hands were in my hair. Only then could I return
to the world, illuminated by the taste of him in my
mouth—"thick, white, sweet, exuding the piercing smell
of camphor," as it is in the books.

He used to tell me, "You are beautiful." After every period of separation, as though shocked by the fact, he'd say: "You're getting more beautiful. Widowhood suits you." I never thought myself a widow, neither in his absence nor in his presence. I'd smile and think of Garance's response in *Les Enfants du paradis*: "I'm not beautiful, I'm simply alive. That's all there is to it." I'd say nothing, but he understood the silence of my smile.

He would encircle my wrist with two fingers and say, "This is what comes to mind when I think of you: closed and open. It's something rare." He'd squeeze harder as he explained to me. With him, the discoveries never ceased. Everything was new to me. This was what he called "the nutcracker." I had to look it up right away in the dictionary of sex.

Long after he'd left me I still shuddered with the feeling of him inside me. I'd wait for the moment when I could slip away from others to be on my own, then close my eyes and fill myself with him all over again. I never told him.

He would say, "You don't talk much," and I would content myself with a smile. I talked to myself. I had become accustomed to talking to myself. Even with him?

He would close his eyes as though he were reviewing a storehouse of images: "What I see drawn before me is the furrow down the middle of your back that ends in two deep dimples. Two curves above your waist, and then your buttocks. Beneath the dome lies the Silk Road. Did you know that?" he would ask. And I would reply frivolously, "I cannot see what you see."

"I'll bring a camera next time, and you'll see what I see," he'd answer, as if he were sure to astonish me.

One day, after an absence, the Thinker asked me, "Do you think about me?" I said, "Yes." "So it's love," he said. I fell silent and didn't answer.

The Thinker was incapable of walking next to me without putting his hand on my backside and caressing it through my clothes or directly on the flesh. I'd yell and move away, saying "You're crazy! We're in the street. People can see us." I was a coward and my sexual freedom only expressed itself in practical terms when I was far from others. "You attract people's attention when you move away. In fact, they see nothing. Nobody will look at us if you keep walking calmly," he would respond, putting his hand back on me. I'd gasp in spite of myself and cling to him. And I would forget the strangers' eyes.

He'd start looking for the doorway to the next building so that he could draw me inside, kiss my lips, suck on my tongue, and feel my breasts. His boldness flustered me, but I was thrilled by the game. I took to walking next to him, my eyes searching with his for that doorway where I could kiss him, suck on his tongue, and feel his body.

One day the Thinker wrote to me. A love letter. I said to myself, How can he use the word "love"? I avoid it as much as I can, with him and with others. I do not know love, I know desire. Love belongs to a world of occult mysteries that is beyond me, and I have no desire to chase after it. Desire—my own or another's—is something I know. I can touch it, see it, smell it, experience its effects and transformations. It alone takes me by the hand to lead me toward my unknown spaces.

Love is for the soul, desire for the body. I have no soul. This idea haunted me before I discovered that there was a time when women were denied a soul.

When I was young I couldn't find my soul. When I grew up, I couldn't be bothered to look for it. "I have no soul"—the sentence became engraved in my memory and I started to live my life through it. I knew that I was body alone, that I possessed nothing else. My body was my intelligence, my consciousness, and my culture. He who desired my body loved me. He who loved my body desired me. This was the only love that I knew, and the rest was literature.

When the Thinker asked me at the beginning, "Is what is between us just sex?" I didn't answer. I didn't say to him, "I love only with my body. I have no other way of expressing love."

Before the Thinker, my public and my secret lives ran in parallel. As a little girl, I'd learned in school that two parallel lines never meet. Some wits claim that in the schools in Saudi Arabia they add the words "unless God wills," but that's another story.

The parallel lines of my life never met, just like it says in the books on architecture. The Thinker came and confusion set in, like in Saudi Arabian schools.

The change began within me. I carried him out of my secret life and introduced him into my public one. I'd think about him, look for him, yearn to see him. I was scared. He had stepped into my everyday life, and it was not what I had bargained for. Equilibrium is my lifeline and to break it meant that everything would change. That is not what I wanted. I had wanted to control my own life with the skill of a great director. Now that I had departed from the script, the plot was running away from me, the pages of the script turned before my eyes but I was unable to grasp them.

I look at my face in the mirror and I remember. He said, "after love, your eyes turn dark and your skin is illumined, as though there were a light beneath your pores." "All women are like that after love," I would reply. He would rub his face between my breasts and nestle there. I would tighten my arms around him to force him closer against my breasts, the better to feel him.

I contemplate my body and I remember. The first time he entered me, he praised the glory of God. I smiled. He pressed me to him, naked and hot. He kissed me and I forgot to laugh.

In my dream, the Thinker was waiting for me and I burned to be with him but the people around us would not allow it. I told him the dream. He wasn't amused. "As you are in life, so you are in the dream—powerless, incapable of doing anything for me." He spoke solemnly, looking deep into my eyes. I turned away and pretended to be absorbed by the passers-by, trying to ignore the boiling of my blood and the pounding in my heart.

Was I starting to get scared?

The night the Thinker stole into my dreams, I knew that our story was beyond my control. The abyss opened before me and day after day I watched it grow wider.

The Thinker wrote me a love letter: my heart was blind and I was afraid.

Before the Thinker, men entered my dreams only long after they had left my bed. None of them, ever, had slipped from my bed into my sleep. They had to be left to mature in my secret caves for a time before they could come to me in my dreams and enliven them. I needed time as my accomplice to recreate them as stories that kindled my imagination, as words that restored my balance. The

Thinker, however, would steal away from my bed and enter my dreams: he was going too far, too fast. He came to me. I awoke.

I was scared.

Third Gate

SEX AND THE (ARAB) CITY

F ollowing the shock of the first discovery, I continued to read whatever books on sex I came across in Arabic, wherever my curiosity led me. I waited years, however, before starting my systematic reading. That began when I first went to work at the university library, where I stumbled upon a long list of erotic books in Arabic. I started reading carefully, one by one. Was it not part of my duties to know the contents of the library's holdings?

My professional conscience was indefatigable. The book remained invisible, carefully concealed under a plain wrapper or hidden behind another and, from a distance, I appeared to be a very serious and very studious person, utterly absorbed by her research. The moment a student approached me the clandestine book would disappear. I would attend to his request and go back to my reading. Whenever a new book was added to the collection in what I considered my specialization, my appetite for discovery would lead me straight to it. As the years passed and my readings accumulated, I became an expert on books on erotica. A secret expert, of course.

One day, what had been hidden was ushered into the light of day. The director of the library came to me, and said, "The Bibliothèque Nationale is preparing an exhibition entitled 'The Hell of Books.' You know, those volumes that are placed on a special shelf in the library to keep them out of sight. The exhibition will be accompanied by a seminar on erotic literature throughout the world. What do you say? They're looking for someone to write a study of ancient Arabic books on sex. What do you say? I suggested your name to them. What do you say? They're waiting for you to accept so that that they can go over the details with you. What do you say?"

What did I say?

I thanked him, warily, for his confidence in me. The whole business had been a secret game, or at least a discreet one. Now it seemed it was turning into an academic specialization. I pictured myself reading one of my favorite passages from one of those books in a loud voice in front of a gathering of scholars. Would I be transformed into a doctor of eroticism? A pornologist? And if I began to giggle? Was there something comic about the whole thing?

"The seminar will be held in the United States. What do you say? Did I tell you that it's being organized in collaboration with New York University and that the exhibition will transfer there after it finishes in Paris? Are you aware that the Americans have become interested in everything Arab and Muslim since September 11th? What do you say?"

What could I say—about their newfound interest, or about September 11th? Nothing.

I might find some points of convergence with the Americans if they started to show an interest in the Arab sciences of coition.

A shy man, perhaps the director thought that, away from the library, he might find some points of convergence with me. In a manner that he didn't dare even allude to.

The director's face was not one to inspire much levity. Why then did he behave as though he was making an indecent proposal? I nodded in agreement. How could I not, when he talked as though he were asking me to write a study of the Seven Readings of the Koran? With the same complicit seriousness, he gave me the name of the person in charge. "Get in touch with him and you can agree on the details. What do you say?"

Secret reading had become a scholarly specialization. Long live progress, and the abolition of our taboos in deed, word, reading, writing, and seminar topics.

My secret readings had made me believe that the Arabs were the only nation in the world that considered sex a blessing and thanked God for it. Does not the Assiduous and Learned Sheik Muhammad al-Nafzawi, may God have mercy upon him and be well pleased with him, opens his *Perfumed Garden* with "praise to God, who placed man's greatest pleasure in the cunt of women and that of women in the penises of men; for the cunt finds no ease, calm, or rest unless entered by the penis, and the penis finds none except through the vagina"?

Did not the Arab authors believe that one of the benefits of copulation (over and above that of the perpetuation of life) was that it provided a glimpse of paradise? Coition necessarily drew our attention to the promised pleasures of the afterlife—"for to tempt one with the image of a happiness that does not exist would be pointless."

So, we are to taste in this world some of the rewards we shall experience in the next? This is what economists call "a production incentive." Sex is a scent along the path leading to paradise, a place where: "the penis never wearies, the cunt is never absent, and desire never flags. There is, in the desire for copulation, a sort of wisdom that, in the long term, engenders pleasure; it directs our attention to the promised pleasures of Paradise and spurs us to seek them in order to deserve them. Observe, then, God's blessings, and how he has created from one desire two lives, one manifest and one hidden—the life of man through the survival of his progeny, and the hidden life, which is the otherworldly life. For this pleasure that is ephemeral stimulates the desire for a pleasure that is eternal and perfect."

Even when the body lost its ability to respond to the demands of desire, the Arabs went to great lengths to trick it into attaining its pleasures, not just by means of strengtheners and energizers, requiring lengthy and complicated preparation, but also by more elaborate stratagems. Thus the Caliph al-Mutawakkil, for example, "loved to have intercourse frequently but became too weak to move. So a basin was made for him that was filled with mercury and his mattress was spread upon it, the very one upon which he fornicated. The mercury allowed him to move without his having to move himself."

If I were to see the Thinker now, I would tell him, "sex is divine grace and my study will begin with this idea. It will be the basis for my study on Arabic sexual literature."

Why does the image of the Thinker return to me these days, mingled with the ancient texts?

The decision exploded inside me like a bomb. I realized that I would be doing what I had put off doing for so many years. I realized that I would be making public what I had kept secret for so long, the truth buried deep inside me. I realized that I would be making my parallel life public, would be bringing my little pile of secrets out into the light, tearing away the last curtain to reveal the darkened stage.

I realized that I must do what I had been postponing until now: conjure up the Thinker after an absence; write him in next to those Arab authors whom we had loved together.

The moment I started writing the study the decision exploded inside me as though the Thinker had taken hold of my hand and forced me to do what I had never dared to do before, forcing me to say out loud what I had only ever murmured in silence. He was forcing me to write my secret story with him.

Everyone I met in this society of pious dissimulation warned me off the topic. Why? The ideas themselves were not the reason. I was free to formulate ideas as I liked. The problem was the raw words. They were dangerous, I was told. They incur censorship. It seemed they hadn't been following what was being written these days in the Arab World. They hadn't awoken to the fact that of the forbidden triangle only two angles remained—religion and politics. Sex had fallen through the censor's sieve or, let us say, the sieve's holes had grown wider.

A few days later I met up with Sahar, a scholar at a Parisian university. Without preamble, she asked, "Is it true you're working on a book about love as seen by the Arabs? There are lots of books on the subject. Have you read André Miquel? Have you read about platonic love? About Qays and Layla? About . . ."

I interrupted her enthusiasm with deliberate rudeness.

"I'm writing about sex as seen by the Arabs."

She fell silent for a moment and hesitated before continuing. Then she asked, "Have you found a publisher?"

"I haven't looked for one. I'm writing a study as a contribution to a seminar on the subject."

"You're making a mistake. You should start looking for a publisher now. Subjects like that sell."

"I didn't choose the subject. It was proposed to me and I accepted. It's an academic study."

"Academic?"

"Right. On ancient Arab erotica."

"I've read some translated into French. Very beautiful."

"I'm writing in Arabic and relying on the original texts."

"In Arabic? In that case the problem will be the censor. There's no problem in using explicit words in a foreign language. It's a different matter in Arabic."

"The texts exist, are published, and are sold in the bookshops. I'm not making anything up. I told you, it's a study. I'm not the first."

"And if it's banned?"

I replied scornfully: "Then I'll be famous."

"All writers these days dream of having their books banned so they'll become famous."

And why not? If the censor is prone to such stupidity, why not?

Fourth Gate

ON WATER

Possessed by the study that I was writing, happy with its publicly acknowledged status, I spoke about it at length to everyone, with great pleasure. I requested leave from the library, gathered up my books, and fled Paris for Tunis. I wanted to write the opening pages in my world, the Arab world. I felt a physical need for that world. For the language and the people. For the streets and the gardens and the tastes and the scents and the light and the sounds. For the faces and the bodies. A need for the sun and the sea. A need for the hammam, the souk, the masseuse, and the scalding water.

When I think of hammam, I think of sex. My mind associates the one with the other, irresistibly. Why? Is it the heat that wafts from my pores? Is it the beating of the blood in my temples that seems to herald sensual delight? I leave the hot room and my body appears rosy before me. After the bath I become beautiful, like after love. The Thinker used to tell me that every time.

"The Sufi al-Junayd wrote: 'I hunger for coition as I hunger for food.'" I have a physical need for water, semen, and words. The three things I need in life. I cannot exist without them. Each helps to organize my confusion and accompanies me through my days and nights. When I open my eyes in the morning, I am as disjointed as a puppet, I neither see, nor hear, nor understand. I stumble to the bathroom. I stand under the gush of the shower and the parts of my body gradually start to assemble themselves. The water collects me, like a sorcerer manipulating my strings and uncovering my innermost self. I recover my senses and my powers. I become supple, ready for life.

I stretched myself out on a slab of stone in the hammam, as though crucified. I divined the bodies of the other women through the hot mist. My eyes were wide open. I watched the steam depositing droplets that merged together on the domed ceiling, waiting to fall. They taught us in school that Newton discovered gravity watching an apple fall. What would I discover?

Would I discover the gravitational pull of the Thinker? That was no discovery. I had known it and lived it.

After all those hours in the hammam I could not help but think about him, could not help but know that I was ready for love, ready for the Thinker. He used to tell me, "We shall meet tomorrow. Be ready." And I would reply, "You know that I am ready for you, always."

I am the cleanest woman in the world, not from love of cleanliness but from a passion for water. The same passion will make it impossible for me to die anywhere but in an Arab city by the sea. Water is the first element. My first element. I felt the truth of this on my skin, even before I read it in books. Even before reading this Hadith from the Prophet to his daughter Fatima, on the eve of her wedding to 'Ali ibn Abi Talib: "Wash yourself ever with water; thus, when your husband looks at you, he shall delight in you." I washed myself with water; thus, when I looked at myself, I was delighted.

It was not so long ago that the hammam was where the mother of the groom would evaluate prospective daughters-in-law. What better place to see a woman as she really is? It was a flawless method, with no cheating and no deception. The bride like Eve in Paradise. As she really is.

I turned over on my back and in silence the masseuse continued her hard scrubbing of my skin. One of her colleagues asked me if I understood Arabic. Did I look so much like a foreigner—an orientalist?

There, in that traditional hammam, there was no place for fake folklore—no cushions of velvet or oriental perfumes. There were only the women, the tiles, and the water. And that smell that I could identify among a thousand, coming to me from Damascus, the city of my childhood. In those years, I went only rarely to the women's baths as my mother was as far as could be from such rituals. Our young neighbor took me there sometimes. I remember the steam, the oranges, the bread with oil and thyme. A family hammam for women and children of the kind you see in certain Arab films. Now the oranges and the thyme had disappeared. Only the smell continued to cling to the place. I like to return to the past through memory—but only through memory.

I stretched out on my back and the masseuse rubbed my body with the coarse loofah. Earlier, in the hot room, she had given me a bucket of water to soak my feet in. Then she came to collect me. I stretched out on my belly, my favorite position. She rubbed hard and I followed the movement of her hands over my body. Little by little, she moved upward from the soles of my feet . . . A light touch from the Thinker's fingers, moving between the two dim-

ples at the base of my back, was enough to ignite a flame
in my belly and my breasts. That was in the past. She
rubbed hard and I closed my eyes to the naked bodies of
the women as they moved around the warm room. A
mother and her three young daughters. A woman with her
elderly mother. The foreign woman with her small breasts,
on her own, like me.

For me the hammam is associated with pleasure, with
sex. Not because of the nakedness so much as the stories
on which I was raised.

Fifth Gate

ON STORIES

S tories. And more stories. Stories of women. I had heard so many, and then forgotten them. Of love and jealousy. Of women clothed and unclothed. Of sleep and waking. Of divorce and marriage. Of those who fell in love and those who were unfaithful. Unspeakable chaos, and relationships so tangled that it would take an astrologer to unravel them. Women's stories that resembled men's stories—I was attracted to both. In every Arab city, the same stories. Stories of the kind you wouldn't suspect in this world of *taqiyya*, of dissimulation, where people have learned to live their sexuality, as with other dangerous domains in their lives, with pious duplicity.

I am stretched on my back at the hammam in a working-class neighborhood of an Arab city. Men come here in the morning, women in the afternoon. Yesterday, I met Rajaa at the mixed-sex hammam of the Grand Hôtel. We were alone in the relaxing room following our treatment; there are few customers at that time of year. I was drowsing, insouciant and languid. Two men came in, and stretched out on the velvet cushions in the midst of the sumptuous Oriental décor. They were smoking and talking in loud voices. I glanced at Rajaa, who was quietly drinking tea and we understood one another. Our nap had been interrupted, so we fled together to the sands of the beach, far from the noise and smoke.

Our neighbor in Damascus used to take me with her to the cinema. I was the solution that she had arrived at with her husband to allow her to move with limited freedom in a city where she knew no one. In the darkness of the cinema I would see her head swaying rhythmically to the sound of the songs of Farid al-Atrash, whose face filled the screen, and it amazed me. I was too young to understand such stolen euphoria.

One day, I told Sulayma about these outings with our young neighbor. She concluded, categorically: "She must have been using you as a cover for her assignations."

"No!" I yelled in protest. "No. She couldn't have."

She interrupted me: "In the darkness of the cinema, could you tell who was sitting on the other side of her?"

This time, I was the categorical one. "You don't know what Damascus was like in those days. I used to go with her to the three o'clock showing. The only people you'd see there were groups of women with their small children. Your tendentious conclusions have no basis, can't you see?"

She replied with a smile. "Why are you defending her, I'd like to know. Have you considered the usher, for example?"

I wasn't defending my young neighbor. Vigilant, ever on the alert, I wanted to defend the images impressed upon my memory. I couldn't stand the idea of anyone chipping away pieces of my old stories and changing their meanings behind my back: I was defending my personal history.

At a later point in my childhood, one of our uncles, a ladies' tailor, came from far away to sew clothes for all of us, our neighbors included. "He didn't spare a single woman," as my sister put it. That young neighbor with whom I went to the cinema was one of those he fondled. He spread the fabric over her, and then followed her curves of her figure with a sure hand. She blushed through the entire spectrum from pale pink to bright crimson; she wriggled, smiled in embarrassment, and said nothing. I watched the two of them while waiting impatiently for my turn to try on my new dress. I heard my adolescent sister yelling on behalf of our neighbor, "Uncle, that's enough! Stop it! Uncle, enough!" Uncle never paused in his work.

I was young when this dressmaking relative came to visit. The stories would unfold in front of me but I wouldn't understand much. All I know is that, after a long discussion with my mother behind the closed door of their bedroom, my father convinced his relative to curtail his visit and return to his wife and children in his distant city.

My adolescent sister was the instigator of this sentence. Years later I learnt that she had come to know of secret meetings that went much further than touching and hues of pink, a story of secret trysts. A story between the skilful tailor and a well-educated spinster neighbor of ours, who devoted herself to raising her nephews, as their own mother was ill. My sister feared that there would be a scandal and told my mother, who in turn also grew fearful. In order to get rid of the dangerous guest she invented an abridged version of the real story, one that was innocent but convincing, for my father. As usual, he believed her.

Some years later, when the neighbor in question was well over forty, she ended up grist for the gossip mill once more. She ran away with a taxi driver who worked the road from Damascus to Beirut and who was much younger than she. She had travelled with him a number of times accompanying the nephews on visits to the Lebanese branch of the family. She fell in love with him and he with her and they decided to get married. She knew full well that her brother would never agree and would consider the very idea an unforgivable crime: who would look after the children, with their mother sick in bed?

The family (rich, traditional, and hailing from the countryside) covered the story up. Quite simply, they erased the existence of the lovesick runaway, and her very name was consigned to oblivion. The news was passed on, in whispers, among the neighbors. In our house, my father would shake his head and repeat: "Ibtisam. Who would have thought it?" My mother would glance in the direction of us little ones, so that he would understand and shut up. So he kept his thoughts to himself, but could not stop shaking his head.

I was very young at the time. I confess I had forgotten all about her. Over the years she went right out of my head. I try to recall now what she looked like—dark, small, silky hair cut short, dressed simply. There was consensus among both sexes that she was sensible, skilful, intelligent, and a clever housekeeper, but she had been unlucky. They would crease their lips with pity at that last adjective. I remember her above all as kind. We younger children liked her because she would kiss us and give us a few coins whenever we saw her.

How did her story end? I don't know. Her elopement with her young sweetheart was not the end; that was the beginning.

The next time I go to Damascus I'll ask my sister for the details.

On the garden steps at Rajaa's house, in front of the Seville orange tree and the roses in bloom, we exchange stories, mixing up the eras and places and characters. Her husband is away on business for a week, the two boys are at summer camp, and she is on vacation. She's all mine.

Her husband was a colleague of ours at the University of Damascus. They fell in love and were married immediately after graduation. With Rajaa, everything is simple, and with me, it goes without saying, life is complicated. We were so different and others always marveled our friendship, and at how solid it was. I was the mischievous, cheeky one; she was sweet and obliging. She was at peace with the world, I was rebellious. We had always chatted a lot, but we had never traded secrets. We were content with allusions to our private lives; the rest we could only guess at. She knew only what I had openly declared about my life; I knew nothing about her secret life.

The scent of jasmine and the rustling darkness. The black cat on the wall opposite listens to our hushed words and fixes us both with a steady stare.

"And Maysaa? What's her news?" I ask.

"I saw her last summer when I was in Damascus. Her husband died some months ago and her two sons are studying in the United States. I think she'll go and settle there."

"She's living on her own?"

"Her mother's with her."

Maysaa's mother was the tragedy in her life, or so I used

to think. I remember how Maysaa's tears mixed with mine on her wedding day. We were together in secondary school. Day by day I shared with her the story of her love for a relative of hers in Beirut, a boy about her age, of a modest background, and penniless, as her mother said. Her mother had an engineer in mind, scion of the family, who was more than twenty years her senior. Maysaa's mother was a strong woman, and Maysaa was fragile and irresolute. She would whisper her refusal of the match in the morning and receive the would-be groom with a smile in the evening. We used to walk home from school together, each of us hugging her school bag, and she would tell me of her troubles. She told me how unpleasant her fiancé was: he hadn't even tried to touch her hand, and he was miserly. She told me how she would sleep with her beloved but, she emphasized, she wasn't crazy, she knew where to "draw the line." Each new story increased my hatred of her mother. A few weeks after the results of the *baccalau-réat*, Maysaa was married in the neighborhood church. I was there. She said goodbye to me and embraced me. We both wept and our tears mingled. Her mother's smile trumpeted victory.

I went to visit her not long after she came back from her honeymoon. She was expecting her first child. She rubbed her belly, which hadn't grown big yet, with a contented circular movement as she talked about the new house, the sumptuous furniture, her husband's family, and the costly presents. The tears of love had evaporated and the bride's face was radiant with happiness.

I said nothing. I was trying to understand how she had been able to betray her tears. I was trying to work out how not to betray my own. I was trying to forget her past words, her beloved, and her ambitions, and I made a pact with myself never to succumb like her.

"Draw the line," said Maysaa. I was to hear this from many women, first in Damascus, and then here in Paris. All of them were careful to "draw the line." I didn't understand were this line was located. Or, more truthfully, I refused to understand.

I heard about it from a friend of my sister's, Hyam. Tall, slim, with long naturally blond hair and large, round eyes, Hyam had a sweetheart who was at least ten years older than her. She'd tell her mother she was studying with my sister at our house. In actual fact she only stayed for less than a quarter of an hour. Then her sweetheart, Muhammad, would come by in his car to take her to his house. She'd do everything you could think of with him, then "draw the line." The irony was that she was proud of her open relationship with her mother and would tell her everything. When I expressed my disbelief one day and said, "Everything?" she stammered and said, "Everything except Muhammad." We used to read over his letters to her together and deconstruct them like a literary text. Muhammad was madly in love with her. The years passed and finally they got engaged and then married. Afterwards, neither my sister nor I heard any more about her.

Here in Paris I heard about "the line" from one of my neighbors at the university dorms. She was a Lebanese who was doing her doctoral thesis on a Lebanese poet with one of the orientalists. When her lover, a well-known Egyptian artist, visited Paris, she'd pack up her things and go and stay with him in his hotel. Their story was known to one and all. Despite this, she'd held fast to that good old line because she didn't want to sully her family's reputation, above all that of her two young brothers.

"Nobody knows what the future holds. You take a risk by living a relationship openly in front of everyone. What do you do if a relationship doesn't end in marriage?" she would warn, and I would listen, looking all the while at the extraordinary painting that had pride of place in her neat room, a painting by her lover. Could he have depicted her like that if she hadn't "drawn the line"? I wondered, believing that I knew the answer.

I would come across this expression in most of the stories I heard. It was easy enough to set off down the path, but once you came to that line, which way would you go? Arab women speak bitterly of men's double standards in their intimate relationships, and the men talk with resignation of women's schizophrenia. Is there any way out? Will we forever be yoked to such a fate?

I avoided seeing Maysaa again, pleading studies and exams as an excuse. Then I went abroad . . . I sometimes hear news of her from mutual friends. She had two boys and no girls, and lived happily ever after.

"Isn't her mother sick?" I asked.

"Very. Maysaa is looking after her. I don't think she'll live long."

"She'll be on her own?"

Rajaa shrugged her shoulders and said nothing.

Perhaps the next time I visit Damascus, I shall get in touch with Maysaa. I could even stop by and see her. I could try to understand her. Rajaa, trying to find mitigating circumstances for Maysaa, responds quietly that the explanation is obvious, while I insist that I cannot find any justification for her behavior, even after all these years. I know very well that humans are self-justifying creatures, but I know too that time changes nothing. On the contrary, it emphasizes and reinforces our characteristics and our choices.

When I'm looking for stories I go to Rajaa's girl friends. Every conversation we have eventually veers off in the direction that interests me. There's no end of stories and I'm like the fires of Hell, insatiable.

Yesterday with Rajaa, as we were walking on the beach, her friend Haniya, a professor of sociology, was telling us about a book she's putting together about the letters exchanged between her parents. About the love story that only ended with the mother's death; the father died soon thereafter. Thirty years of rare mutual understanding. We spoke of love, marriage, children, endurance, infidelity, and divorce. A typical intimate conversation.

After a silence during which we couldn't hear even our own footfalls, Haniya's voice resumed: "Once I wanted to go abroad in connection with my work and my husband refused absolutely. I got angry. I decided to ask for a divorce, despite two children and ten years of shared life. I went to my aunt on my father's side to tell her of my woes, and my determination. She gave me the following advice: 'Listen, my dear. Spite the devil and don't make a fuss about it. Go to the bathhouse and get pretty. Then go and meet your husband and make love with him as if it were the first time. The next day talk to him again about your trip . . .'"

Haniya stopped talking.

"And?" I prompted.

"I went abroad."

Only a few words, and an indecipherable expression on her face.

None of us said anything. What similar stories of our own were we recalling in silence? How many decisions, great and small, have we forged in bed? How many disputes had we resolved through such methods of persuasion?

Our generation was doing nothing new. There were many situations of the sort in the books of my masters. Al-Qali, an eminent Arab encyclopedist, writes:

Some ill will came between a man and his wife, and they shunned one another for a few days. Then he jumped on top of her and took her. And when he had emptied himself, she said: "Shame on you! Every time there is ill will between us, you bring me an intercessor whom I cannot refuse." And in another tale a woman, mourning the passing of her days and particularly her nights with his "upright judge," said to her aging husband: "The one who used to resolve our disputes has died."

Rajaa turned to me and said, "You want stories of love? I'll take you to see my friend Nadia, she knows all the stories for miles around."

"I want stories about sex," I said.

"We use the word 'love,'" said Rajaa, giving me a mischievous look. "We rarely use the word 'sex.' But is there a difference?"

Nadia was waiting for us at her house. Rajaa had told me a lot about her. She opened the door to us semi-naked. Just a short, diaphanous pareo knotted at her chest and falling to the tops of her legs. It was obvious that she didn't feel any shame about her body, and there was nothing to feel ashamed about. With the red rose tied in her hair, like a girl of the islands, she was beautiful. She spoke and moved freely. And her freedom made her even more beautiful.

As soon as we went inside, the telephone rang and she pounced on the receiver. Her lover was ringing from France. She gave us a wink before continuing the conversation, which sounded as if it were going to be very spicy.

"He's a lot older than she. His lamp's running out of oil," whispered Rajaa with a laugh.

I liked Nadia. I liked her confident movements. She read us extracts from her diaries where she described their torrid trysts. Rajaa winked at me: "Don't believe it. These are her fantasies. I've seen him. He's very old and he can hardly move."

But I wanted to believe. Nadia was frank about her age and that of her lover, and burst out laughing, too. Could she not live a love story at her age, and after all her years as a widow? She left the room to fetch the tea and chocolates. I looked at her and it occurred to me that any man who crossed her path could not help but fall in love with her.

"Any man? Or any man of her generation?" Rajaa asked, with irony.

"Do you want to hear the latest?" asked Nadia.

"Take care," Rajaa warned her, laughing and pointing to me. "She knows all the stories of the town, even the rumors. Your story will have to be really fresh."

"I'm certain you won't have heard it. This young actress went to study in Paris. She got to know a French producer as old as her father. Very rich and very influential. Married and with children older than she was. He fell in love with her. Her skin was brown and smooth and she was passionate. He went crazy over her. She drove him insane. He promised he would produce a blockbuster with her as the heroine, and he kept his word. You know what this generation's like, everything all in a hurry. She wanted to be a famous actress, and he was obsessed with her youth. He would follow her to Tunis whenever she went there to visit her family. The last time he came here, he had a heart attack."

"And then what?" I prompted her.

I knew the story couldn't end there.

"He died. They were together. He was making love to her. He died on top of her. Someone asked if he'd died before he'd come or after. No one knew the answer."

"And then what?"

"And then what? And then what? You want more? It was a scandal. I told you, the whole town was talking about it."

I hadn't heard about the scandal, but I'd seen the film. The poor young thing did indeed have the lead role, and the critics praised her promising talent and scintillating presence. She was a star. Who cared about the scandal? It would melt like a grain of salt and the film would remain, with the glory of the road that had opened up before her. A practical generation for a practical time. Then, too, the scandal had a spice about it that stimulated the imagination and, like a magnet, would draw people's hearts to it. This was something I knew very well.

"A scandal with bells on it," as they say in Egypt. The bells are chiming from your buttocks, and the noise is deafening. I listened to Nadia and it occurred to me that the actress's butt was cause for alarm, and that her bells would certainly catch the eye.

I recalled this adamant assertion: "There is no sex in Egypt!"

"There is no sex in Islamic society!" Words of a young French writer whose novel had been quite a success two years earlier; that had, indeed, won a literary prize. The words belong to the book's narrator, who travels to Egypt to take part in the Cairo Book Fair, nourished by his orientalist delusions. He travels in the footsteps of Flaubert and his women . . . and fails to find what he's looking for, of course. Gone are the Nubian maidens the writer had encountered in the nineteenth century, "adorned with necklaces of gold pieces that reached to their thighs and with belts of colored pearls over their black bellies." In their place are women wearing hijabs. The cultured traveler is traumatized to find that Flaubert's Levant, the Levant of 1847, has vanished. All that is left is September 11th and the days of Islamic jihad. The only woman to fulfill the hero's expectations is an opportunistic Francophone Moroccan who works at the French embassy, of whom it is said that she is the most beautiful woman in Cairo. And yet he will reject her advances out of loyalty to his beloved who is waiting for him in Paris. After this pitiful adventure, long conversations with Francophile Egyptians and with travelers even more disappointed than he himself regarding Muslim men and women, the young novelist is forced to conclude: Islam and sex do not mix. A universal truth discovered by a French novelist in the matter of a few days. The earth is round, and there is no sex in Islamic society. This catchphrase echoes another: "There is no sex in the Soviet Union." The first was proclaimed in nostalgic tones by a writer returning empty-handed from his travels, the second by a puritanical communist in a television interview. In either case, blind propaganda prospers in ignorance, whether real or feigned.

"Why didn't Sulayma come with you?" asked Nadia.

"She has guests," lied Rajaa, in a neutral tone that convinced no one.

Nadia and Sulayma do not get along, but I love them both and their personal conflicts don't concern me.

I love Lebanese Sulayma, who married a Moroccan diplomat and now lives with him in Tunis. This is the virtue of Paris: it allows the Mashriq and the Maghreb to meet. If you make the acquaintance of such a couple, there's a good chance that they'll have gotten to know one another in Paris.

I love Sulayma. I enjoy her company and love listening to her stories. Arab and French stories about her first lover, and her second, and her third, and . . . and . . . about her lovers whom she cannot count and half of whose names she cannot remember. Are these are stories from before her marriage—or after? Society demands that the page remain blank, to be marked only by the scribblings of the husband.

"He came to see me at the student residence," relates Sulayma. "He was Lebanese like me, tall and beautiful, fair-skinned with black hair. A playboy, every day a new girl. The men were jealous, and the women were mad about him. He was doing a doctorate at the Sorbonne, though he didn't finish it, of course. In fact, he didn't do a thing, except pursue his sexual conquests.

"He lived at the student residence like me. I met him a couple of times with other people. The presence of my Palestinian lover did not stop him flirting with me openly. One day, he came to see me in my room. It was summer and Paris was at its hottest. He'd no sooner sat down than he declared, 'It's hot,' and took off his shirt. Then he said, 'It's hot,' and took off his trousers. He told stories about his Argentinean girlfriend who was jealous and watched him all the time and made his life miserable. I talked with him and responded verbally to his stories but kept my distance while I watched the striptease act that he was performing in front of me. I was curious as to what would follow. I kept talking to him as though he were wearing a tuxedo, when in fact all he had were his white boxers. He said, 'It's very hot,' and took off even those, and stood there as naked as the day he came out of his mother's belly. The difference was that he'd come out of there as a little child, and now he was a man with all his male attributes. Imagine!

"He took hold of his member and said to me, 'See? My girlfriend's crazy. She's so jealous of me she puts a mark on it with a pen and inspects it when I come home, to make sure it's still there.' I was on the point of telling him to give her an indelible marker next time but I didn't. I shook my head in commiseration, looked at where the mark was, examined it, and made a show of surprise. He stayed naked as a worm for more than twenty minutes, strutting about in front of me in my room, standing at my window, and looking at the paintings on my wall, while I watched him with cool curiosity and kept up an ordinary chatter with him. In the end he said, 'I feel ridiculous,' and put on his clothes. I nearly agreed with him. He left me with two light pecks on the cheek, like an ordinary friend, and that was the last time he came to see me in my room."

"And then what?" I asked, as usual.

I always want the stories to go further.

"Then nothing. We became friends. He got married and I got married. He got divorced and I got divorced. He got married again and I got married again and went abroad. Sometimes we run into one another when I'm in Paris. He knows my second husband. When we meet, he gives me a hug and a kiss. Ordinary friends."

"Amazing! Friends? After something like that?"

"Why not?"

"Have you ever talked about it?"

"Once he said to me, 'Do you remember the day I visited you at the dorms and you took your clothes off?' I told him, 'No, sweetie, I didn't take anything off. You took everything off and then put everything back on again and left.' 'I did that? Was I such an idiot?' 'That's exactly what you said at the time,' I answered."

"Was he testing your memory or did he want to rewrite the facts of history? Did he think something like that could be forgotten? If so, he really was an idiot."

"What's even better is that I told the story one day to a mutual friend, and he laughed from the depths of his heart and said, 'You know, I was jealous of his beauty and even of his wit—every day with a different girl, and each one more beautiful than the last. He was giving me a complex. It reassures me to hear how you treated him: yes, there is a woman on this earth who can say no to him! Now he's just like the rest of us.'"

"Another idiot. It seems there are lots around like that."

"When it comes to women, they lose their heads."

"Like we lose ours when it has to do with men," I continue, and our laughter mingles.

I look at Sulayma the artist, whose paintings abound with sensuality and bright colors. Plump naked women, with heavy breasts and even heavier buttocks, women overflowing with curves. I look at Sulayma as she talks and all I see is her beauty, her smile, her lightheartedness, and her indifference to the image she projects. Perhaps I love her because I don't have her courage, child of dissimulation that I am. I have drawn my own image, and have always preserved it jealously. I have never spoken of my secret life, or my hidden stories, either orally or in writing.

I have never dared. I know now that this won't be the case for much longer. I smile to myself with a certain mischief as I continue the conversation.

Sixth Gate

On the Masseuse
and Her Adulterous Husband

T he first time I saw her, I failed to notice the beauty of her features.

I met her at the spa. The receptionist led me to her but, in her presence, she kept her eyes lowered. With a sure and certain step, she walked ahead of me into the massage room. She raised her eyes and looked at me only once she had closed the door. And only then did I see her smile, and hear her greeting: "You're Arab? You are most welcome. Where are you from? We don't get many Arab tourists here at the spa. You are most welcome."

She came to the point very quickly.

"I divorced him after he got out of prison."

"Prison?"

"Yes. For adultery."

"Adultery?"

"The police caught him with a woman."

"A woman?"

"I myself went to the police station and asked them to come."

"The police?"

I repeated her words, with a mechanical slowness.

"He thought I was here, at work, like any other day. But the *patron* saw that I was tired and gave me the day off. I returned home unexpectedly and saw them there together."

"You saw them together?"

"Through the window. I didn't go in. I just saw them through the window. What a shock! From that day I've had this hoarseness in my voice, as though someone had tried to cut my throat and something got caught in my windpipe. Even now, three years on, I still feel as if I'm choking whenever I think of it."

"Did you know her?"

"No, I didn't. God forbid. A loose woman. A slut. God forbid. What are they called where you come from?"

I almost said, "Where I come from they call them whores," but I held my tongue and settled for fallen woman. It's almost the same thing.

Her fingers were moving over my back. I couldn't see her, only heard her voice.

"He did that to me after five years of marriage. Our love story had been very intense. And in the end? He betrays me, in my own house, in my bed. Thank God that here in Tunisia they don't take adultery lightly. He was in prison nine whole months. He deserves what he got."

Adultery?

"Any relation between a man and a woman who are not bound by the ties of matrimony and in which complete sexual contact occurs." The word "complete" is a story unto itself, the definition becomes conditional. What, then, constitutes incomplete? The Imam Khomeini himself, believe it or not, states the following in his book of fatwas: "kissing, sexual contact, embracing, and further acts of pleasure that do not involve contact between the sexual organs of the male and the female are not to be considered adulterous, and incur other punishments; such chastisement remains at the judge's discretion."

Hearing the hoarse voice of the masseuse, I imagine tears welling in her kohl-rimmed eyes.

I thought of the oft-repeated stories about Monica and the cigar and this question, asked insatiably by the host of a French television show of his guests: "Should sucking be considered infidelity?"

He could have put this fundamental question to the Ayatollah during his French sojourn. He would have given him the definitive answer on this delicate matter.

In one of the old stories that my mother always used to tell us, she spotted my father in the street, walking with a strange woman. He didn't see her. He was too absorbed by the other woman. My mother quickly crossed the street to avoid running into them.

The details of the story might change, but her voice as she told it was always the same: full of pride. I was young and would listen to her and picture the scene as though I were watching it on a screen. My father laughing, his arm around the waist of a beautiful woman wearing a pillbox hat. She leans her head on his shoulder with a coquettish smile. A whore? In the eyes of my mother she couldn't have been anything else. I imagined my mother, who was also beautiful, quickly weaving her way through the cars to the other side. Her head down, not wanting my father to discover her there.

A melodramatic moment open to multiple interpretations, you might say.

There was a time in which I would attempt to decipher its various meanings. Now I no longer want to understand. I content myself with reviewing the images in my head and going over them again and again, like a cinema-lover watching a cult film.

A simple case of adultery? As though adultery were something simple. As though one could commit adultery just like that. As though it were nothing. Such misguided thoughts reveal an ignorance of adultery's precise rules and regulations, rules that cannot be bent. It has ever been so.

The first condition of the adulterer is that he be a youth of tender years and sweet of smell, the reason for this being that sweet smells bring the woman into heat and intensify her desire; also that he wear clean and hand-some clothes, make frequent use of the bathhouse, and employ henna on his hair, as well as using a twig to pol-ish his teeth, and oils; that he have among his acquain-tances an old woman to act as a go-between; that he be soft of heart, quickly moved to tears, capable of weep-ing whenever he wills so that, when he finds the oppor-tunity to speak with his beloved, he may complain that passion has destroyed him. Should such conditions be fulfilled in the man and he be alone with a woman, he will find her more biddable to him than his own feel-ings and closer to his desire than his own breathing.

These conditions applied to the man only, as if the author were aware that women are always ready for pas-sion. If all the conditions are met, the adulterous act can be picked like a ripe fruit.

These conditions applied to the man only. In the woman, one sought outward signs of desire.

If he speak with her, her eyes never leave him, a blissful look overcomes her, she plays with the hem of her dress or her wrap as though she were about to pull it over her head; she stirs the earth with her toes or touches it intermittently with her big toe; she bathes her child and dresses him in finery, combs his hair, rims his eyes with kohl, and introduces the child to him; she mentions him often and talks about him with her female friends and neighbors; grows weary and changes her mood for no reason should she cease to have news of him; and befriends his wife, if he has one, and visits her frequently; and if she sees something at his house that belongs to him she takes it in her hand and makes a great fuss over it, and if she finds his bed, she lies down on in and squirms about on it.

For the Arabs, desire was all-powerful. The universe of lovers was subject only to its reign. Desire answered to nothing but its own laws, the same laws for men and for women, which neither marriage nor children changed. The basic scenario was scripted for its two heroes alone. All those who surrounded them—spouses, children, friends and neighbors—were no more than extras who could do nothing to prevent, or rein in, the lovers' lust; they could at best be catalysts that ignited the fires of desire or helped to express it. The leading roles belonged to the lovers, and those around them were bit players.

"Here, no one knows I'm divorced. You know how men look at a divorced woman. They crave her. They hover around her and try her out. I don't want problems. I'm raising my daughter on my own. There's no one to stand by me. My father told me, 'Forgive him. He made a mistake and he won't do it again.' My husband came too, begging to be allowed to return home, but I refused.

When he got out of prison, he came weeping and implor-
ing me."

"How long was the sentence?"

"Nine months, because he was married. And three
months for her. That's the sentence for adultery in our
country. Thank God I have my daughter. She's everything
in my life. I've been living for her alone for the past two
years. I work for her sake. I have no one to stand by me.
There's no one to help me."

Now, there is a civilized country where human rights
are respected, even in cases of marital infidelity. Nine
months for the married, and only three for the unmar-
ried.

A civilized country indeed. Prison, sure, but no flog-
ging, contrary to what is prescribed by the Koran: "The
adulterous woman and man shall each receive one hundred lashes." Starting with the woman, naturally. A truly
civilized county. I had a very close call.

Her fingers massaging the soles of my feet, I was unable
to concentrate enough to do the math: how many years
would I have to spend in prison if on each occasion I were
caught red-handed?

If they had caught me with the Thinker every time we
met, we would have to spend our lives behind bars. And
what if they had caught me with the others before and
after him? My life, no matter how long, would not have
sufficed. I would still owe the law years and years after my
death. Though I wouldn't be alone. My jail would be overflowing, all my acquaintances would be there with me.

All of them? Let's say, most of the people I know would
share their company with me, for varying periods of time,
each according to how clever he or she had been in hiding

their crime. The only innocents are those whose crimes have not yet been discovered.

In flagrante delicto, as with the husband of the masseuse, is the precondition for any punishment, without which it becomes a difficult business. Rumors and accusations are not enough. A'isha, the Prophet's favorite wife, was accused of adultery, and the Prophet set down these conditions of proof:

> Summon four male witnesses who saw the sexual act in detail, namely, the entry of the man's penis into the woman's vagina in the manner that the kohl-applicator enters the kohl-container or the bucket the well.

How can such conditions be met when the act itself is essentially an illicit and thereby clandestine one?

Two lovers were caught one day in the library's toilet. The director general wanted to fire them, but a union representative was quick to ask for a meeting in which he appealed to the Prophet's inalienable conditions in cases such as this. After examining the facts the director, convinced, withdrew his call for their dismissal.

It occurred to me that the husband of the masseuse would not have gone to prison if these conditions had been applied to him. All she had seen through the window was two forms: no bucket and well, no kohl-applicator and kohl-container. Had the policemen really caught them in flagrante delicto? Well of course! They knew their religion, in that country, just as the union representative friend, in the heart of Paris, knew how to convince the director general of the library.

*

"Did he marry again?"

"No. He lives by himself like a dog. Pardon my expression. There's no one to take care of him, to cook for him. He sends his clothes to the laundry. He's like a dog. I have my daughter, who's the whole world to me."

"Does he see her?"

"Yes, he sees her. I don't say anything bad about him in front of her. He's still her father. I don't want her to hate him. He is still her father whatever may have happened."

Her voice has grown even hoarser, and her fingers are now on my leg. The scent of the jasmine oil fills the booth. Laying face down, I can still smell it even though my nose is pressed against the sheet. I turn my face a little and see a beauty spot on the edges of her round face.

I close my eyes and surrender with genuine innocence to the soothing rhythm, the practiced fingers, the scent of jasmine, and the old images that throb in my naked body. I try to catch hold of them before giving way.

Walking beside me in Saint Germain, Sonia asked, "Fathiya confessed that she's been trying to seduce you for years without success. Is that true?"

I didn't answer, merely gave a smile.

"Why?" she insisted.

"Why is she trying to seduce me?"

"No. Why do you refuse?"

"I don't know," I replied, shrugging my shoulders to make light of it.

"You don't find her attractive?"

"Maybe."

"You're afraid to break your fast with an onion? That it will ruin your pleasure?"

I didn't say that. Fathiya is not an onion, and I held back a smile of complicity as Sonia laughed mockingly. "It's an experience that we have to have, even if it's only once. For the pleasure of discovery," she went on.

I didn't tell her that I hadn't yet finished exploring the world of men and, so far at least, was not in need of additional complications.

"You might behave differently, with another woman," she insisted, craftily.

"If, by some miracle, I desired a woman, I would be the one to seduce her."

"That's just overstatement, as usual. I don't believe you."

"I don't need to be believed."

"Don't you ever stop playing games?" she said, looking at me out of the corner of her eye with assumed exasperation.

"Perhaps. The day when there are no men left on earth . . ."

"Or the day you find yourself with Fathiya on a desert island."

"Fathiya or anyone else," I replied wickedly.

In the street, the sounds of our laughter mingled and rose.

The old books of erotica have passed down *The Stories of Huba of Medina*, a remarkable woman who spared neither men nor women. The story goes that to her daughter she said:

Above all, never forget to moan when fucking, and know that once in the desert I gave such a cry as to terrify the camels of 'Uthman ibn Abi 'Affan, may God be pleased with him, so that they ran away, and to this day have not been rounded up.

Our grandmothers were worthier than us. They made the best of both worlds.

A man was told that his wife loved women. He replied, "Indeed. I have ordered her to so do for it purifies the opening of her sex. Thus, when she has contact with the penis, she knows better how to appreciate it."

And what about our grandfathers? May they all rest in peace.

"In the interests of comparison, some women have said, 'Fucking a man is healthy, fucking a woman is discreet.'" This is the fruit of deep wisdom that I do not have. If the masseuse had been a man, my mind would have been full of fantasies and my body feverish.

A French novelist wrote, "I was a lesbian for three months." Could I do better than that? I should write, "I was a lesbian for only three minutes." It seems we're not lesbians by nature, neither I nor the French novelist.

The physicians have written that this malady is an inborn characteristic of women. Unless the habit of raising slave girls under the same roof from earliest childhood is the cause. As they mature, they continue therefore to desire what they have known. The same may be true of prostitution. If this Sapphic malady is acquired, it shall be easy to eliminate. If it is inborn, it shall be long and difficult to treat.

The masseuse is a woman and her touch is professional and does not stir my imagination. My blood remains cold, and my mental images calm. My taste for men is not the only reason, surely. Plenty of women, past and present, have "made the best of both worlds." Up to this point, I have seen only men. Full stop. Fathiya used to melt with desire as she said to me, "I love you," but her declarations only made me laugh. Why laughter? To escape the embarrassment? For fear that I might accept? To make fun of her use of English whenever she spoke of emotions? She had a refined intellect, so she would laugh with me, as though she knew perfectly well that I was deferring my reply.

My masseuse went on in a low voice, as though revealing the secrets of the universe: "Monique, the Frenchwoman, the client before you. You saw her as you came in. I think she's had a hard time with men. When I told her my story, she said, 'There's no trusting men. I will never trust another one.' Something happened to her, it must have. I asked her but she just shook her head. Something must have happened to her, I'm sure. She will tell her story some day. She has to tell it. She still has a few days left here, she'll tell me her story. She only ever wants me to give her her massage. She asks for me by name. She gave me her address in Paris and took mine. She's sure to tell me her story. She said: 'Don't trust men.' She's right. Of course she's right."

I couldn't give her the same advice. Why are women always talking about trust?

Hisham, the Prophet's servant, did say: "A man came complaining to the Prophet and said, 'My wife does not reject the hands of those who touch her.'
The Prophet advised: 'Divorce her.'
The man said, 'I love her.'
The Prophet replied, 'Then take pleasure in her.'"

I have grasped this simple lesson: I take my pleasure with men and they take their pleasure with me. Full stop? I do not ask of them either love, or faithfulness, or devotion, or any commitment that might limit their horizons, close their eyes, or zip up their flies.

By the time Monique tells her story, I'll be gone. I'll have said goodbye to this sea, this country, this masseuse. By the time Monique tells her story, I'll be gone, back to my life. Do I need to hear her story? History repeats itself. I know the words by heart.

She will say she found out he was betraying me.

She will say he came to her weeping because he loved another woman and couldn't bear to lie to her any longer and so he had to tell her the truth, no matter how painful.

She will say that other well-intentioned people had already informed her, and when she confronted him he confessed to the crime and thanked her because she had relieved him of the burden of lying, so heavy to carry.

She will say, after all those years of marriage she had discovered that he preferred men. That he had a lover. That everyone knew except her.

She will say, he packed his bags and left the house.

She will say she cannot bear for someone to betray her trust.

She will say that men do not deserve our trust.

Will she talk about her loneliness? Will she talk about her search for another man? Will she talk about the nights out with her single girl friends? About the matrimonial agencies and singles clubs and Internet dates?

Men do not deserve our trust?

As I arrived, Monique was coming out of the booth. A dyed blonde with a smile stuck to her face, which shone with massage oil.

"Next time Monique comes from Paris, she'll bring me a face cream. She made me swear to ask her for whatever I want. She'll give me a call as soon as she arrives. The first day she asked me to put her in touch with someone who could give her a hair removal treatment with sugar. You know the sugar treatment? You use it in your country too? She wants to remove all the hair on her body—legs, arms, armpits, and the face too. Everything. I sent a friend of mine to her room at the hotel and she was very pleased. It costs her a lot less that way than if she goes to a beauty salon. She wants to go to the hammam in the city center, too, not to the hotel bathhouse. I'm going to go with her on my day off. I only get a half day off each week. My daughter's with my sister in the capital. She insisted on staying with her for the school vacation. She's a help to me. I love your accent. It sounds so nice. There's a serial from your country that I watch every evening. It's fantastic. I've forgotten the name. Excuse me just a moment, I've got to go put the music on and I'll be right back."

A song from the Gulf that I don't know precedes her return:

Ah, you beauty, who, when you came,
Cast all others in the shade!

You looked down upon us
And of all that light
Yet more light you made!

I haven't listened to Arabic songs since the time of the Thinker. Songs from the Gulf are new to my ear.

Why does he haunt my thoughts so insistently after all these years?

Seventh Gate

ON THE ECSTASIES OF THE BODY

I opened myself to him with all my senses. I gazed at him. Savored his smell. Hung on his every word. He would talk and I loved his words, words that ignited my desire. He mixed the poetry he recited and the words of his own pleasure in his cries. When I drew close to the abyss, he would control the rhythm of my movements. This is torture! I would cry in protest. Later I would understand, and learn in turn how to hold back my quest for the final shudder, the shudder that left me breathless, smeared with honey and semen; I would learn how to hug my freshly picked pleasure like a heartbeat between my legs.

The first time I saw him. We were with a group of friends, men and women, at a dinner party. *Mezzé* and Lebanese arak and chatter and political discussions and risqué jokes and laughter. He was doing the rounds, saying goodbye to everyone. It was still early. When he got to me, he gave me a polite, distant kiss, and suddenly the smell of his body reached me: the smell of desire. I breathed it in, and realized that we would meet again and that this smell would fill my lungs and the pores of my skin.

"Whence springs love?" asks Ibn Arabi.

"I love what fills me with light and increases the darkness deep within me," answers René Char.

Between the question and an intimation of the reply, I moved ever closer to the Thinker, becoming more aware of the dangerous game that was defining itself in the space between us.

Ever since I met the Thinker, even after all these years, not a single day has gone by without my thinking of him. I cannot desire a man without thinking of him. I cannot read a newspaper without thinking of him. Every day, something reminds me of him.

What? What reminds me of him?

Every detail of my life is linked to him. With him I learnt to swim slowly, to sink beneath my own undertow, toward the bottom, calmly, confident that he was with me, and that when I opened my eyes I would find him there.

Open my eyes? I didn't really close them. I tried to remain wakeful, alert. To see him, and be seen by him.

The first time I saw him. I was in the metro. I was reading a satirical newspaper. I raised my eyes and saw him staring at me. He was sitting opposite me, talking with friends. I went back to my reading, but I was distracted. There was something in him that called to me; something in his look that called to me. Our eyes met again and that stubborn, exploratory look was trained on me. We got off at the same station. We each went our own way with a last, lingering look. But I didn't have enough time to register that look so that I might recall it, and try to decipher it.

The first time I saw him. He was sitting in front of me at the political conference I had come to attend. He was with a group of people that I knew. A mutual friend introduced us and from that point on he did not leave me. He stayed by my side, and I felt good. For two days we did not leave one another; we parted only in the evening, each returning to our respective life.

He gestured to his throat. "It grabs me here," he said at the end of the second day, for my ears only. Had I heard him correctly? When he repeated this words, I knew that I had been waiting for them. I almost gave that half serious, half mocking laugh that I use to avoid the issue. But then I didn't dare. I didn't dare play with him the game that I play with others. His presence was so complete that it obliged me to answer him. I felt dizzy. How did I know that I had to make my decision at that instant, or lose him?

I didn't want to lose him.

The first time I saw him. I was with the Palestinian film director. He was in Paris for just a few days and we had agreed that we'd meet at a café in the *Quartier latin* known for its Arab clientele. He was with two other men at the next table. I heard something in Arabic about the situation in Lebanon. I could see his face; the two others had their backs to me. He was opposite me, talking somewhat angrily, and his eyes never left mine. As one of his friends stood to leave he recognized the Palestinian filmmaker. Greetings and congratulations all round, and they put the two tables together. He sat next to me, and from that point on, never left my side. He talked and laughed, as though a sudden happiness had taken him unawares. His bare arm brushed against mine. How many times did his bare arm brush against mine? "I'm sorry. I don't usually behave like that, but something stronger than me made me move closer to you," he told me later, when I was in his arms.

He was forever reciting poetry. Whole poems that he'd learn by heart. He'd read them to me and I'd imagine he was writing them over again, for me alone.

Was poetry one of the keys to my body?

Poetry was there between us. He loved me through the poems of others. When he was traveling, he would phone me to give me the name of a collection and a poem. I would look for the poet, read the words, and know that he was with me.

Pessoa, Cavafy, Char, Michaux; others I didn't know. I became like him. I would learn the Arabic poems that I loved by heart and recite them for him, and only him.

Was poetry always there between us?

With him, I started writing my short poems once again, and it became an opening ritual for each of our encounters. He'd ask me about my words. In silence, I would offer him the poem and he would read as though discovering the dark side I concealed with frivolity and laughter. He would discover things that I didn't dare reveal even to myself. In silence, he would fold the paper carefully and put it in his pocket.

Was my body one of the keys to poetry?

The first time I saw him. I was at a Book Fair in an Arab capital. I was filling in for a colleague who'd fallen ill at the last moment; the director had chosen her to represent the library. I went in her place, somewhat grudgingly. When a representative of the fair came to welcome the five people arriving from Paris, he was next to me. His questions gave off a magnetic force, under the mask of legitimate curiosity. A form of conversation without end. He opened up to me, and I to him. He told me how he'd seen me at the airport, and how he'd watched me from his seat on the plane. It was as though he knew me. I told him the same story: it was as though I knew him. Our encounters do not end, and the body is always the preamble. The body was the basis of our story.

Every morning, the Thinker accompanies my nudity. It's enough for me to look at myself naked in the mirror to remember his words about my body. About my breasts, my ass, my sex, my skin, my smell, my color.

I recall his words and I shudder. I recall his words and his touch and his gaze and I shudder.

I recall and I shudder, but I want to forget, to get on with my life.

The Thinker used to ask me, "Do you know what it is I love about you?"

I would give him a knowing look and I laughed.

"No, it's not what you think, even though *I do love your dirty mind*."

Laughing, he repeated the well-known English phrase.

"I wasn't thinking anything. I was just waiting for the answer."

"I love two things about you. Your free spirit and your Arabness."

"Never in my life would it have occurred to me that a free spirit and Arabness could be the height of sex appeal," I replied, with a light-heartedness that tried to hide the pain racking my consciousness, as the words penetrated deep within, to re-emerge, later on, letter by letter.

Now I recall his words and I shudder. Now I recall his words, his touch, his gaze, and I shiver.

I recall them now and I do not want to forget.

I want to remember.

I want to write.

Multiple scenarios; identical first encounters. The sudden discovery of the other, the looks exchanged, the words repeated, the nervous laughter, the unintentional touches, the anguish of the moment of declaration. How is it that we re-create all these details differently each time?

Which of these first times was the Thinker's? All, or none of them? The minor details differ but the story remains the same. I love details, in any story; their color gives a new meaning to each story.

Every new man is a new story. Which of these stories was the Thinker's?

The Distant One sent me an email, in English, with a stupid joke called "The Woman and the Bed":

When she's eight, you take her to bed to tell her a story.

When she's eighteen, you tell her a story to take her to bed.

When she's twenty-eight, you don't need to tell her a story to take her to bed.

When she's thirty-eight, she tells you a story to take you to bed.

When she's forty-eight, she tells you a story to avoid having to go to bed.

When she's fifty-eight, you stay in bed to avoid her story.

When she's sixty-eight, if you take her to bed, then that's the story.

When she's seventy-eight, what bed; what story? What devil of a man are you?

A stupid joke of the sort men tell one another in an attempt to forget the trap they've fallen into. What I found interesting were the two alternating motifs—the bed and the story.

In my life, one has led to the other, and vice versa. In my life, they have been intimately linked, and I oscillate between the two.

In my life, I have been addicted to beds and stories. Every man is a story and every story a bed.

I don't want to lose the bed. I don't want to lose the story.

On the bed of stories I sway and strut.
I touch the sky with my fingers
And dig valleys in the desert of my soul.

"I would use *firash* for 'bed,'" the Distant One wrote to me after I'd emailed back to him the translation into Arabic of his joke. "Why do you use *sarir*?"

I replied, "The *firash*, for me, is for sleeping and sickness, childbirth and death. The *sarir* is for pleasure. *Sarir* is from *sirr*, or 'secret.' Two words which have the same root. Desire is secret. Pleasure is secret. Sex is secret. Sex is the secret of secrets. That is why in my mind it remains linked to the *sarir*, even if I do it in a lift."

"Have you done it in a lift?" asked the Distant One in his reply.

I pictured his thick eyebrows raised in avid curiosity.

"Not even on the beach!" I replied, shortly.

I love secrets. These stories that no one knows but me. These stories give my life meaning. An entire life that belongs to me alone, that I share with no one. It's enough for me to close my eyes to taste the *honeyed juice of pleasure*, as it is called in the Hadith, the sayings of the Prophet. It's enough for me to close my eyes and the image rises before me, the sound, sight, smell, touch, and taste. It's enough . . .

Could I go on living without them? Could I wake up every morning and find the strength to begin a new day without them? The answer comes clear and sharp as the blade of a sword, and I am not afraid.

In the long spans between stories, I live off memories, confident that the coming days will bring me my new story.

I could not merely wait, because I don't know how to wait. Nor could I precipitate them. And then? I often asked myself this question, without ever really looking for an answer. The answers, like the stories, came of their own accord, in their own time, as ripe fruit falls from the tree.

Eighth Gate

On Arab Dissimulation

T hat morning I was working on the section on aphrodisiacs and the same evening I found myself surrounded by my male friends whose conversation revolved around that very topic. They were swapping stories about an Egyptian artist who tried some sort of Syrian Viagra. His member remained flaccid, while his head started to swell up. Terrified, the girl who was with him fled. He was scared, too, even more than she, but didn't dare call the doctor. Instead he called a friend, who told him to wait a little, long enough for the unexpected symptoms to go away on their own, and not to do it again.

In a study on sexual impotence among men in the Arab World, I read disturbing figures regarding the fantastic dollar amounts spent on Viagra and other love remedies, as they are called in the advertisements I get daily over the Internet. This brought to mind the characters in the last novel I read by Rashid al-Da'if and how they take Viagra like aspirin.

Why do they expect Viagra to rescue them from their misery? A collective sexual misery, present even in our relationship to our traditions. Why bother with Viagra! All one has to do is read those old manuals of Arab eroticism and apply their prescriptions. "Results guaranteed!" said the old authors. "Try these remedies and you'll obtain miracles!" Arouse women and excite men. Lengthen and thicken your penis. Constrict the vagina and make it tastier. True, some of the ingredients, such as red bull's pizzle, white cockerel's brains, and wolf's spleen, are difficult to obtain; but pepper, spikenard, musk, ginger, grape juice, and oil are available to everyone.

Take lukewarm water and massage the penis with it until it turns red and becomes erect. Then take a piece of thin parchment and put hot tar on it and wrap it around the penis. If you do this frequently, it will grow larger and longer.

Before undertaking such measures (and this is my personal advice), you'd better make sure you have the number of the nearest hospital handy.

The publisher pulled out his cell phone and started reading a joke that had been sent to him by SMS, the latest technology to be put at the service of the lewd joke. I've already heard this particular joke, but I go ahead and laugh with the others. I knew a certain Elie, who, every day on his cell phone, got fresh jokes about Hayfaa Wahba and Nancy Ajram, our archetypical bimbos and the butt of many a saucy Arab joke. He'd learn them by heart to tell them later. The latest jokes generally reach me via the Internet. I read them and generally forget them, with the exception of those that include word play.

I sat listening as the intellectuals of our society of dissimulation spoke, and mentally I took notes. The publisher was telling a new joke. He didn't read it off the cell phone this time. He'd memorized it. They laughed and exchanged opinions. I didn't say a lot. I was content, as usual, with laconic comments and expansive laughter.

"Viagra has rescued us all," said the Enumerator. "Both ourselves and our honor. God bless the people who discovered it and their lab assistants. They ought to be nominated for the Nobel Prize. They have performed a service to all humanity, women and men."

The Poet told another amusing story and they all laughed heartily.

"Do you know why they classify Viagra now as a cosmetic and not as a medicine?" asked the publisher.

I had heard the joke so I settled for polite laughter.

"Because it restores our honor!"

"I've never used it," said the Enumerator, disapprovingly. "I've bought it for friends in Arab countries. Every time I ask one of them, 'What do you want me to bring you from Paris?' the answer is, 'Viagra.' Imported Viagra is very expensive over there, while the locally produced variety is cheap. And apparently it's good, results guaranteed."

I listened to him detailing the prices of the different brands and their degrees of effectiveness.

"You say you don't use it yet you know all about it?" said the Spinning Top.

"I've bought it for friends. Nothing more than gifts, I swear. They're the ones who tell me about it."

In the Thinker's day, there was no such thing as Viagra. I desired him. He desired me. We didn't need the products of any foreign laboratory. Our bodies were enough.

What would the people sitting around me think if they

read what I'm writing? What would they think if they discovered I had broken the social contract? That I had violated the Law of Dissimulation that everybody applies? What a scandal! "So that's what she was hiding behind her laughter? I was sure there was something going on, that under that impenetrable mask there was a wanton woman of the first order. I was sure of it . . ."

How many of them would insist that they had always known what was going on?

Mocking laughter arose. All of them were men. At first they didn't dare use the *ibahya* words—salacious words, as they termed them—in front of a woman. But I laughed loudly, not the least bit embarrassed. So they ventured into territory meant for men only. They would forget that I was there, or pretend to forget, which is what I wanted. I made full use of the maxim, "When a man and a woman meet, there is always a third: the devil." At present there are four men gathered around my reassuring social personality, and I am the devil.

"In the past my sugar level was so high that I couldn't do a thing without Viagra. Now after my diet my sugar's gone down and I don't need any stimulants."

I looked at the Poet and it occurred to me that he had indeed lost a quarter of his weight. Still, I wasn't convinced that he could make love without a little help.

Everyone ordered seafood dishes. I remembered something a doctor had written in the magazine *Elaph* about a soup known as "Poor-man's Viagra":

An Egyptian invention whose secret is jealously guarded by fish restaurateurs and itinerant fish-vendors. It consists of an arbitrary mixture of seafood such as mus-

sels, winkles, crabs' legs, and bits of shrimp, plus a little boiled fish and lots of chili pepper and spices, and
every newly wedded couple in the coastal areas is
advised to take it and places blind faith in it. Necessity
being the mother of invention, the people there, to
whom the minister of health has so long denied Viagra,
came up with this wonderful soup, which warms their
bodies and restores life and energy to their limbs.

The friends sitting around me must certainly know the
miracle recipe; they don't need me to help them choose
what will make them feel good.

One day the Activist arrived at the library wearing a
smile from ear to ear. I raised my eyebrows the moment I
entered his office, and I knew he had something to tell me.
"Close the door," he said in a whisper. "Would you
believe, yesterday I tried Viagra for the first time. It really
is extraordinary. May God bless the inventor. And may he
repay his good deed a hundredfold and welcome him into
Paradise."

Then there was the Director, who went on and on that
"the erotic must by definition be revolutionary." He would
hold up the magic box that he'd ordered directly from the
United States and announce in front of everyone, "I have
the box. All I need now is the woman."
When we replied, "How about your wife?" he would
answer truculently, "I'm not going to waste it on my wife.
In my entire life I've never seen her satisfied. My wife? The
very idea!"

We would laugh, eat, and drink in our restaurant in
Paris. I had always seen them together, and always without
their wives—even in their own homes, in their own countries.

Where were their wives?

I thought of a scene in a film by Fatih Akin, where the
German hero says to some Turkish men as they are about
to head to a brothel, "Why don't you fuck your wives
instead?" They blanch, and are so offended that one of
them jumps on the offending German to beat him up. In
the room next door, meanwhile, the wives are making fun
of their husbands' performance in the marital bed.

At least these friends of mine don't make a show of
virtue, abstinence, or decorum. Freedom of speech is
undoubtedly a form of sexual freedom. Who was it who
said that words meant nothing and bore little relation to
the act? Not true! To talk about sex is to indulge in it.
Words are a component of sexual energy.

I remember another neighbor in Damascus and her stories full of double entendres, her equivocal words, and my
mother's embarrassed smile as she listened to the woman,
whom she considered brainless and mad. I was too young.
I didn't understand most of her allusions, but I could
sense the sort of nimbus that surrounded her like a saint's
halo, a wave of heat that burned anyone who drew near.
She frightened the women, and fascinated the men.

The funniest thing is that my friends resort to foreign
languages when they want to use sexually explicit words.
Obscenity is mitigated when spoken in a foreign language.
The embarrassment they feel using those same words in
Arabic evaporates. In English or French, they can pro-
nounce any of them with the greatest of confidence.

Ninth Gate

ON LINGUISTICS

I am a creature of language. Each passing day confirms the fact. Language sets traps for me; it compels me to listen to its voices, to gaze upon its colors, to sound its depths. This is why I love dictionaries of all sorts. I use them to excess, and my questions about language are never-ending. No sooner do I utter a new word than I am trying to trace it to its roots in order to understand its origins, its derivatives, and its various shades of meaning. I even try to invent new words in a language that is mine alone.

Yesterday the Traveler shared his motto with me: *Je baise, donc je suis.* He spoke in French, in the language of Sade. "I fuck, therefore I am." I took it to be a joke, a play on words, and repeated it after him.

When speaking in Arabic, the Traveler uses the passive form of the verb: "I get fucked." This deprecating form is something that surprises me about him, as he comes off as an inveterate philanderer, at least in his stories. It occurs to me that I love the word when it is unadorned, free: to fuck. Period.

I fuck, therefore I am. Why can't I say it, or write it, in Arabic? In Arabic, in this day and age the word "fucking" is banished. The word is a sin, though the act itself is legitimate.

All this hypocrisy brings to mind the words of al-Jahiz, one of the ninth century's greatest writers:

> Some of those who are given to asceticism and abstemiousness feel disgust and shrink back if the words "cunt," "cock," and "fucking" are mentioned. Most men of this sort turn out to be as lacking in knowledge and magnanimity, nobility of soul and dignity, as they are rich in falseness and treachery. These words were invented to be used. It is nonsense to invent them if they are then left to go to seed.

I translate the Traveler's "I fuck, therefore I am" into Arabic. I fuck, you fuck . . . I conjugate the verb and search for derivatives. On my computer, the spell-check function underlines each attempt in red. The computer will not admit to knowing such a word! It, too, is programmed for dissimulation. This computer is a shrinking violet! Or, to be more precise, a eunuch of a computer. That has castrated the language. That castrated the computer. That castrated me.

After not seeing each other for some time, I met the Thinker again in a Japanese restaurant. He sat opposite me. He put out his hand to touch mine: "I want you. I want to come inside you. Now." The act of love in words is total and violent. No detail is overlooked—from the burning breath to the shuddering of the body, from the first moistness to the beating heart, from the awkwardness of the first gestures to the shared repose after love.

In the sixteenth century the poetess Louise Labé wrote: "The greatest pleasure, after love, is talking of it." The fact that her existence is contested does not alter the truth of her words.

With the Traveler, much of our conversation was about sex. On our very first encounter, several years ago, he declared: I want you. His desire has never been fulfilled, to this day, but every time we meet, he assures me of the constancy of his desire and describes in detail all the ways in which he intends to satisfy his lust for me. And there are many details; it is an ambitious program. I laugh. Sometimes I let him talk and sometimes ask him to be quiet, depending on my mood. It has turned into a game we play.

At our last meeting, he said to me, "So you reckon we've never made love? Of course we have. We've done better than that, with words."

I smiled and it occurred to me that he might be right. This intimacy we share is something I haven't known with any other man. Or even with any woman. We talk openly about sex. He tells me his adventures in minute detail. And then he urges, "And you? Tell me the last time you slept with a man!"

I answer each time, "I've told you, I don't sleep, I wake."

"Liar. You don't do anything outside of marriage."

He persists in not believing me, harping on the old refrain. I change the subject. I ask him to tell me about his latest trip, or his latest rendezvous with that girl from the Gulf.

"Pretty. Plump. Breasts to drive you wild. But she made my head spin. In bed, she never stopped talking. She sang. She complained. She never stopped spouting nonsense.

She'd give a blow by blow description of what we were doing, like a sports commentator. At first, it excited me, but little by little I started to feel as though her words were a kind of perversion. I tried to shut her up by plastering kisses on her mouth but it was no use. If I stopped to catch my breath, the transmission would start all over again. I don't know how I managed to finish. Ouff!"

I laughed as I tried to imagine the scene. And I wanted more.

"That's the end of the story. Tell me how it began."

"She works in the office of this official I was supposed to meet. She sat next to me at the lunch hosted by her boss. I started flirting, and she let me. I put my leg next to hers under the table and she didn't move hers away. On the contrary, she pressed against me. As I said, she was responsive."

"And the people around you?"

"No one noticed a thing."

"And then?"

"We were on our own and the conversation got more explicit. She told me she liked my boldness. I suggested she come up to my hotel room. Impossible, she said. She was married and had never cheated on her husband."

"And then?"

"She said she'd have to divorce him before she could sleep with me. I said that would take more time than either of us had. I explained to her that as long as she liked me and I liked her, why shouldn't we just enjoy ourselves? She refused vehemently. She went protesting that she loved her husband and would remain faithful to him, but she followed me to my room. In the elevator I kissed her and she went on protesting. As soon as we were in the room, I took off her *abaya*, then the jeans she had underneath, and still she was protesting. I was kissing her breasts and—she protested."

"I get it."

"You wanted details. She was wearing the most beautiful underwear I've ever seen in my life. Pure silk. Absolutely gorgeous. Imagine, her husband's a lot younger than me. Just imagine. She told me it was the first time she'd slept with a man other than her husband."

"Did you believe her?"

Every time a man sleeps with a married woman it's the first time she's been unfaithful to her husband. According to the Arab proverb: Before marriage, the Arab woman says that no lips have touched her own save her mother's. After marriage come her husband's lips. One way or another, they're all virgins.

Siham used to say to every man she met that he was her first, in spite of her marriage and her three children. "Why is that?" they would ask. Because with her husband she knew no pleasure. Because each time he slept with her it was as if he were raping her. He would hit her, and lock her up. She would tell every new man she met that he was the first in her life. She didn't tell me this in person, but her words reached my ears, repeated by several of the men, each of them telling me his version in private.

Tenth Gate

ON UPBRINGING AND EDUCATION

The Thinker kindled a fire. It burned in me for a time, even more so after he left. Was that the price of my initiation? Was that the price of being awakened to life? While waiting for other thinkers and further revelations?

It has come down to us from the ancients that an old woman gave her daughter the following advice, before giving her to her husband: "I will give you a piece of advice, my daughter, which if you hearken to it will make you happy, make your life sweet, and make you fall in love with your husband. If he comes to touch you, gasp and moan, sway your body, and show him languidness and languor. If he grasps your breasts, gasp loudly. If he enters you, weep and speak whorish words, for these arouse sexual desire and assist in strengthening the erection. When you see that he is close to ejaculating, gasp for him and say, 'Come deep inside me!' And when he has filled you, clasp him to your bosom, be patient with him, kiss him, and tell him, 'My master. How sweetly you fuck!'"

My mother never said anything like that to me, not at all. The most risqué thing she ever told me was that angels in Heaven exchanged kisses. The substance of this was that whatever angels did, perforce, mortals were authorized to do. The immediate and practical application of this knowledge was that I had permission to kiss the neighbors' son, but nothing more.

By the time she explained this to me, I had, of course, gone way beyond kissing. I may have laughed out loud, but the thought of angels kissing was engraved in my memory. It's the same thing with all parents: by the time they decide it's the moment to open the door, their children are already out in the garden.

The joke has it that a father says to his son, "You're big enough now for us to talk frankly about sensitive subjects." The adolescent replies, "Tell me, what would you like to know?" We knew more than our parents as young people, and our children will know more than we do. If my mother had read what I have in the ancient books about the kiss, she would not have spoken to me about angels.

Know that the kiss arouses desire to begin with, and then sexual vitality. It brings on erection and ejaculation. It causes the penis to rise, and inflames the woman, especially if a man intersperses his kisses with gentle bites and light pinches.

The only mothers one encounters who are wise enough to teach their daughters lessons on desire are to be found in books of erotica. The advice she gives to her son-in-law will not be less important. In some of the books we find the father himself playing this role and advising his daughter.

Huba did not content herself with teaching the women of Medina "the art of kissing," as prescribed by the books; indeed, she extended her experience to her son. One day, he asked her: "Mother, in which positions do women prefer to be taken by men?" To which she replied: "Dear son, if she is old like me, you should make her lie on the floor with her cheek to the ground, and then insert it all the way into her. And if she is a young girl, you should pin her thighs to her chest, and you will know your desire, and you will have what you want."

Nobody taught me. Not my mother, not my father, and not even my big sister. No one explained anything to me. I studied the theory in books, films, and stories, and by watching men and women around me. As far as practice was concerned, I learned a little at a time, by trial and error. Slowly. I was cooked on a very slow fire; often, indeed, the fire was out. This is not a play on words.

Yes, I started my sex education with writing and films—novels, magazines, films, and serials. Sex education? Well, emotional, at least, with small doses of practical sexual culture and traditional Arab theoretical knowledge. I would have to wait to move to Paris to discover, in French, pornographic films, books, and magazines.

I'm not alone in this ignorance. It seems to be widespread in this age of sexual decadence in which we all now live. I have only to read the questions on sex in the Internet magazine *Elaph* to discover the extent of Arab sexual deprivation. I picture the specialist pulling out his hair as he writes up his findings. How can we talk about sex education when even a rudimentary knowledge of anatomy is still to be acquired?

Yesterday, I happened upon the response of an exasperated physician: "Looking for the hymen in the Arab World has become like looking for a needle in a haystack . . . And waiting for girls to acquire a sound sexual culture is like waiting for Godot." In the fifteenth century, the sheik al-Suyuti authored a book for use by women on the art of making love, but the readers of *Elaph* would not understand a word of it: you may as well give a Neanderthal woman a book on computer programming.

Young men are no better off. Indeed, the number of questions they ask regarding the length of the penis (in repose, erect, at half-mast, real and ideal) would be worthy of the *Guinness Book of Records.*

Every time I venture into this terrain I am more convinced than ever that those who read the old books on sex will be sure to avoid the pitfalls of deprivation. It follows therefore that bringing these books out into the light is a matter of public well-being. We must no longer fear them, but recite from them publicly. We must no longer hide them, but bring them into the open.

This idea will form the conclusion of my study. I shall call for these books to be republished again and again, to be distributed, to be taught.

Hungry for knowledge, I forced myself to explore the word of Arab erotica on my own. I studied our literature assiduously at university, but not one of my professors ever mentioned these ancient texts. When I talk about them, I discover how few of those around me have read them and learnt from them. Several years ago, a literary magazine published the various names used for the male member, as found in one of the erotic tomes. This caused a minor scandal: everyone reads magazines, but books are hidden, reserved for those curious souls who search them out.

During a semi-official banquet, the director of the library, a Frenchman, came out with a witticism: the supine position, he said, was best for both bottles of wine and women. Everyone denounced his shamelessly sexist pronouncement. I reflected that if he could say such a thing aloud he probably didn't think it through. I have learnt life lying down. I don't think I lay down in order to learn, but learning came in concentrated form in the arms of a man.

Yesterday, in my friend Fadia's office, I found myself gazing at her and thinking that her chastity belt was strangling her, that her beauty needed years of rolling around on the body of a man to emerge. He should rub her skin, at length, as though she was in a bathhouse, and only then her self would be exacted from the layers of imposed abstinence. Indeed, he should rub and rub until he had expunged all the bad, stagnant blood. Only then would she make peace with her body and with the world.

I know she's caught in a vicious circle: she cannot learn on her own, and for the moment the man is absent. Her initial education cannot succeed without a man. There is no denying that the man makes things easier, facilitates a woman's apprenticeship. Where is that man? Why has his path not crossed Fadia's? Why has he not seen in her the radiance that I see? Why does she live alone, her fire consuming her?

The scenario is unchanging. Fadia and I begin by talking about work and then the discussion drifts elsewhere. How, that day, did we get started on the subject of sex education? Why did the conversation wander off?

"No one taught us how to behave around boys," she complained. "No one taught us how to decipher that unknown world, a completely different world."

"When we're small, we are taught. When we get older, we teach ourselves," I replied.

They didn't teach us? Indeed. But I did not want anyone to teach me. I learn on my own, filching my knowledge from the one I'm learning from. I learn by pretending to be blind, deaf, and dumb.

Fadia was still talking, but I'd lost the thread . . .

"My mother worked it out only recently. She's proud of us now. She says, 'My daughters are as independent as men. They work and live on their own. Like men.'"

"Like men?"

"She's not used to seeing women lead that sort of life. For her, a woman has to be kept."

Fadia said, "Men are afraid of independent women."

Fadia said, "I'm waiting for a faithful man before I commit."

"Well then, you'll stay single," I joked, hoping my laughter would soften my words.

"Why? There have to be some faithful people in this world. My mother was faithful to my father. My brother is faithful to his wife."

"How can you talk about other people with such confidence?"

"I'll put my hand in the fire if they're not faithful."

"Don't promise to put your hand in the fire unless you're speaking for yourself. Other people, whoever they may be, are full of secrets."

"I'm sure of what I'm saying," she said, over and over again.

I said nothing and she changed the subject. "Women talk too much. We don't know where to stop or how to stop. They didn't teach us."

I told her about the latest episode of the American serial *Sex and the City*. The heroine is making love with a man who is sucking her breasts and murmuring sweet nothings. She reacts: she is not his mother, he isn't a suckling child but a man and so he shouldn't call her breasts by such ridiculous childish names, or suck her nipples that way, because she's a woman whom he desires and not a wet-nurse, and so on. During her lecture, the man's erection droops and finally collapses altogether. In the end, he puts on his clothes and departs, and she sits there with her eyebrows raised in astonishment, wondering why on earth he has left. The viewer understands very well that she should have shut up and left him to suckle her breasts until he was satisfied. Until they were both satisfied. But the heroine didn't understand.

Fadia and I had a good laugh. Then she objected, "Still, it's unacceptable, what he did, absolutely inadmissible."

"You're a lost cause."

I love to learn, but I don't know how to teach others. Nor does Ibtisam, my closest girl friend. We've known each other since childhood, but I don't remember that we ever shared our discoveries. When we were in love, we wouldn't give away any details. On occasion, we'd talk about trivial things where love was involved, but never sex, as if we belonged to some sisterhood of angels. As married women, we've had a lot of children, but again, even today, we never venture beyond mere allusions.

When I see in films nowadays how young girls talk to

one another, I'm astonished by the tone of their shared
secrets, so different from our own as girls. Intimate talk is
a true cultural exchange. I've experienced it at times, but
only with women I've met by chance, in passing. Never
with my closest girl friends, or even with my sisters. Not
even after we got married.

The only woman who ever shared the details of her sex
life was Rihab, and I listened to her with curiosity. Both of
us were expatriates; no doubt this circumstance had
helped certain Arab women to free themselves from the
tyranny of dissimulation, both orally and in writing.

For a program on the French cultural radio station, a
Lebanese director working in France questioned young
men and women of Arab origin on their sex lives. In
dialectal Arabic with simultaneous French translation,
their testimonies were remarkably frank and courageous.
They could speak like that because they knew they were
addressing a Western audience on a Western program. In
any event, no Arab station would ever broadcast such
material.

Rihab broke the Law of Dissimulation with vulgar,
crude language. She came to Paris from a traditional environment and works with us at the library. Her veiled sisters, whose photos were prominently displayed on the
walls in her office, never let us out of their sight whenever
she was relating the adventures of her sex life, as if they
were so many medals. She was a greedy woman, both in
her manner of talking and of eating. I would laugh along
and feign interest. Her stories were always about the latest
man in her life, never more than a fleeting presence . . . and
who could blame them. Rihab was irritating, exasperating,

annoying. Not a single man had ever been able to stay. The first man was seeking a way to obtain legal residence in France for himself and his girl friend; so his arranged marriage with Rihab lasted the time it took for his fiancée to get her papers. Once the divorce was finalized, he went back to his girl friend and married her. Rihab cannot keep track of how many men have followed in his footsteps.

Perhaps it was her stories about men that bound me to her. If I put up with her breathless panting as she delivered her frenetic descriptions, it was, after all, to hear her stories.

"He was at the lady next door's. He didn't even try to deny it. When I accused him of being unfaithful, he answered quite simply, 'I was helping her in the garden. Why are you making a drama out of it?'"

"So why were you making a drama out of it?" I asked, thinking of the series *Desperate Housewives*, with Gabrielle Solis and her gardener lover.

"Imagine! He dared to say such a thing, and look me in the eyes as he said it. And after everything I'd done for him."

In the previous episode, Rihab had fed and housed and married the man, "according to the Law of God and His Messenger" at the mosque in Paris, while waiting for the civil marriage at City Hall, just so that the young student could obtain his permanent residence papers.

"For a year he'd had nowhere to sleep. I rescued him. You know, the first time he came to my place was to do some repair work. I'd just moved in and he offered to help. The moment he was in there he never left again."

Her hysterical giggling punctuated her sentences like so many ellipses.

"He was a student on paper, that's all. He already had a university degree. In fact, when I met him he was selling vegetables at the market, to get by. No sooner did he move in with me than he quit working."

"He wanted to devote himself to you full-time, a perfectly honorable commitment," I said, as serious as could be.

She chuckled again, as though she were recalling happy memories.

"From the first night he came to my bed."

Her words slowed a moment in the silence of the office, then she concluded, "It was my fault. That's what happens when they have nothing to do. Helping the neighbor in her garden! I'll teach him manners. He'll see."

Her expression became nostalgic.

"You know what I like about him? The moment I touch his thing it goes stiff. Ready at any time. He must have had withdrawal symptoms before he even got to Paris. At home, the only thing he had was masturbation. For a penniless student, the prostitutes were too expensive."

I admired her lucidity, her clear awareness of the true dimensions of the story. Rihab was the only one who'd go into minute details. I've never heard another woman go this far. Men yes, whether they're friends or not. Most of them are always eager to tell me their adventures, make me share their experience. And me, always the attentive listener, I've been an ideal audience, with my insatiable curiosity and my inexhaustible laughter.

There was Anwar. We were colleagues, at the first library where I worked in Paris. When we were along in the big shared office, he'd tell me stories about the girls he'd flirted with in the street or at the café or on the bus or in the metro, or even at the library. He was married and, out of caution, stuck to generalities and allusions.

Albert, too, was married. His stories rubbed me the wrong way because they had only one goal, which was to convince me of his immense intellectual, emotional, and sexual prowess, should I ever . . .

Ghadir, a bachelor, shared an abundance of details. His fertile imagination knew no bounds.

In our shared office I was the only woman. Each of the men would take advantage of the others' absence to tell me his real or invented stories. The effect they had on me was identical: I was entertained, I would open my ears wide and laugh. But their hidden strategies, whether conscious or unconscious, never succeeded, for the only thing I ever opened to them was my ears.

It's certain that I learnt a lot from these and other stories. I listened lightly, or at least made a show of listening lightly. My comments were evasive, and if one of them was trying to gauge the effect of his words from my expression, all he'd see was an indifferent gaiety. But I'd make notes of everything I heard, then arrange them, classify them, sort them, and learn. Isn't documentation my profession?

In the midst of a summer heat wave, I return to the old books and to the Thinker, and the world around me is ablaze. Is it what I'm writing that affects what I see? Has the world always been on fire like this?

What's happening? Sex is everywhere. I open the newspapers and find it on the front page and in the headlines and in the weekly supplements. On television. On the radio. In the old days there had only been Brigitte Lahaie, the porn star. Now her gifted disciples have taken over.

What's happening this summer? Everyone I meet has an erotic story to share. As if an invisible spark were setting everyone's thoughts on fire. As though others know instantly what I'm looking for. Are the signs of my sexual curiosity so glaringly obvious?

When did I discover that my curiosity about sex is in fact a thirst for knowledge? I laugh when I read that every woman is the sum total of the men who have passed through her life. "We only learn what we know" was something my brother used to say constantly. From him too I learnt.

The desire for knowledge fuels my desire for men. No, my desire for men fuels my desire for knowledge. To learn, by myself, about desire and pleasure, to learn about others, and about the world. After the Thinker, I began to judge every new man in my life based on his pedagogical qualities above all. The more a man teaches me, the more I love him. After the Thinker, I could no longer put up with a man who couldn't teach me.

For me, the pleasure of learning went along with the pleasure of sex. The center of pleasure and the center of knowledge got mixed up with each other in my head and fused together inseparably. My sexual curiosity grew deeper, deep as an abyss: those who cross my path cannot help but fall into it.

It is said that the virgin, if she be kept too long from copulation, will suffer from a condition that the physicians call "constriction of the womb," which leads to delirium and melancholia in the brain, to the extent that she may be thought mad, though she is not; suffice that she be fucked for the ill to vanish immediately.

*

If I were to say that in front of a militant feminist, she'd declare war on me and accuse me of submitting to male chauvinist ideology.

Fadia. She is a desperate case. "When you're about to shoot someone, you don't tell your life story," says the bad guy in the spaghetti western, before dispatching his chatterbox victim. I repeated this to Fadia but she didn't find it funny. I laughed on my own. I watched her leave the office and shook my head. I suspect she would be capable of taming even the fiercest erection. It's clear that she hasn't learnt a thing. She's at war with her body and with men's as well, and it looks like it'll be a long war.

I'd advise her to read the advice of al-Alfiya, a legendary character whom I consider to be a glorious heroine of women's liberation.

The first time I came across her in my reading, I was awestruck by the breadth of her knowledge. From her life experience she was able to formulate both theoretical and practical teachings, which she presented to the whole world, the female half in particular. She was a genius. May God bless her.

Al-Jahiz, who relates her teachings to us, celebrates her as being the most learned of all the people of her time with regard to the science of coition. What made him admire her still more was that, like himself, she belonged to that school of scholars who speak only of what they know from personal experience, and who will only teach knowledge acquired through the direct observation of real phenomena.

In a gathering of women, questions were asked of al-Alfiya that dealt directly with her domain: "Tell us about intercourse, its types and variations." And the wise woman would reply: "You have asked me concerning something that I cannot suppress and that I have no right to conceal."

The words of al-Alfiya have only reached us through their translations into Arabic. According to al-Jahiz, this woman came to us through Indian erotica, and she became a legend passed on by the Arabs, essentially the men, with a certain degree of fear, envy, and admiration. The legend begins with her name. She was called al-Alfiya, "the thousand," because she had slept with a thousand men. Although "slept" is deceiving . . . As if she had spent a thousand nights sleeping . . . She did not sleep and she would not have let a single man sleep. The books say, precisely, "She fucked a thousand men." Words were exact, among the Arabs of ancient times. There was no business of sleeping or waking. To "fuck" was the word used.

What is the dictionary definition of the Arabic word for fuck? Are there not a number of verbs with the same meaning? It is said that there are a hundred words or more for the vagina, and a hundred more for the penis, but in fact they never have the same meaning: each word is distinct from the others. I did not count them. What is important, above all, is to catch the nuances.

Al-Alfiya's response to the issue is methodical and rigorous: there are six basic modes—lying on the back, lying on the side, lying on the stomach, bending over, sitting, and standing up. Within each mode there are at least ten positions, and each position has a name. Sixty positions, then, starting from the easy ones that everyone can apply to the arcane that would never occur to anyone and that call for the physical agility of an athlete and the skill of a circus acrobat.

Al-Alfiya would explain to her female listeners what it was that made love of women spring up in the hearts of men, what men took pleasure in and what they hated in terms of women's dispositions, and what women had to do to procure men's desire.

If al-Alfiya were among us now, she would write a book about her sex adventures, with her picture, naked, on the cover, and it would top all the bestseller lists and be translated into every living language, and her fame would travel around the world. How could al-Alfiya ever imagine that her legitimate heirs, centuries later, spread over five continents, would not even know her name, when she was the first, the pioneer?

Eleventh Gate

ON RUSES

When the Thinker left, I was as traumatized as a nursing child torn too soon from its mother's breast—in a state of loss, of pain, of perdition, of death. The Thinker was my secret, and I had to live my public life without others discovering that secret.

When the Thinker left, I hoped he would die. I built myself a tomb hidden away in my heart. I had to protect myself. I protected myself by dying. When was I resurrected?

When I was with him, it was easy for me to hide my parallel life. Without him, this became more complicated. My parallel life had turned into absence, a non-life. And yet, I had to keep hiding it. I lived for months like the living dead. I wandered through my life emptied of all life.

I woke, slept, smiled, spoke, laughed, worked, travelled, and met others; I performed all my duties. I lied, I led a double life. I went about my business, moving my body by means of invisible strings, and with the skill of a virtuoso puppeteer.

When the Thinker left, I hoped he would die. I understood then the meaning of a story I had read in childhood: a king asks his daughter to determine the fate of her imprisoned lover. Of the two doors that kept him behind bars, one would lead him to life, in the bed of another woman, and the other to certain death in the jaws of a lion. The story has no ending. It is left suspended, focused on the princess's raised hand as she is about to indicate one of the doors. As for me, I knew without a moment's hesitation which door I would have opened. But the Thinker left without giving me the chance to choose. He left before the end of the story. He left without my seeing the word "departure" blazoned on my horizon. He was the one who chose the door, leaving me to face the hurt.

By day, my Thinker-self would scream its pain alone, far from me. I would hear its deafening screams and I knew that I must not turn toward them or I would collapse like a cracked edifice.

By night, I would return to him and make peace with him. We were united in our loss. I would sleep and wake, my eyes dry as an abandoned well and my spirit drier still.

I armed myself, in order to survive, with the only weapon I had: the innocence of lies.

Time has numbed my pain. One day, a man told me, in the same tone of voice and with the same assurance, "You are beautiful." I smiled. For a brief moment I believed him, and I was brought back to life, jolted back to life as if I had received a charge of electricity.

Years after the departure of the Thinker, I realized that each of us has a Thinker, male or female, one or many, who waits for us in some part of the world to reveal us to ourselves, to uncover our powers, so that we can go further into the labyrinths of our beings.

Years after the departure of the Thinker, I realized that

each of us has a Thinker waiting for that given moment in life, on one of its many roads.

We may lose our Thinker with a word, a shrug, a postponed journey, an awkward explanation, a dull-witted ancestral fear, or for having followed the rules of a game to whose laws we submit.

There are those who live and die without meeting this indispensible Other, who will open doors previously closed to the world.

There are those who live and die like a head of lettuce, wilted and emptied of life; those who never know what it is to be transformed into a burning coal that that consumes everything that approaches it. There are those who live and die without learning the way to their bodies, or to that of others.

How many little coincidences had to come together for me to discover the existence of the Thinker and for him to discover mine, for me to see him and for him to see me?

How many little coincidences had to come together for the moment of the first, decisive discovery to occur? Today, I can count off the moments of our affair as if they were prayer beads, one by one. But the day I met him, I had no idea that I held in my hands the thread of this story. My story.

Years after the departure of the Thinker, there were times I still whispered his name. I knew what he had given me and I was grateful to him. At other times, I cursed him.

Years after the departure of the Thinker, I stopped resisting and confessed.

At the beginning, he used to ask me, "Is what we have just about sex?" and I would avoid answering.

In the end, he no longer asked me.

In the end, he left.

In the end . . .

Years after the departure of the Thinker, a sentence by a German poet that he used to recite to me sprang to mind: "God created Man as the sea created the continents—by withdrawing." Had he withdrawn so that I might be created?

I go back over what I have written about him and it occurs to me that what I have related is not about him alone. The stories have mingled, so too their heroes. Perhaps they all fused together in him, the Thinker. Those who came before him, and those who came after.

When I set off along the tracks of my men, each one takes on the appearance of the Thinker. They have disappeared into him. They have left him their place and gone away. They have surrendered everything to him as I surrendered everything. They have surrendered to him without knowing anything about him. They are gone, and I alone have remained with him; I know the whole story.

I read what I have written and it occurs to me that everything I have experienced was of my own making. The Thinker did nothing but lift the veil on all I had gathered in preparation for life. He came so that I might arrive at meaning. He didn't bestow it on me: I found it through him.

I read what I have written and it occurs to me that I have made the Thinker into an allegory. I have recreated him, but not in my image. I said, "Be," and he was. He was just as my words had shaped him. This image belongs to me; it has nothing to do with him.

Why the Thinker?

The question occurs to me now as I am rereading what I have written. He wasn't the most charming, the most brilliant, the most virile, or the most amusing. He wasn't. He was himself.

He was the Thinker. I read what I have written and it occurs to me that the Thinker was a writer's device, a ruse, and that he never existed at all: that is why I had to invent him.

I understand now what he meant when he said, every time we met, "You are the core of what is between us. You are the source of what is between us." The first time he said it I was upset. Then I became accustomed to the idea, I understood its implications, and made a game of it with him. The story is mine; he is only the subject.

I tell it and play with it according to my will.

Now it occurs to me that, in truth, everything I experienced after the Thinker already existed within me, hidden. I was living with his absence, confident that I would meet him again one day.

I didn't look for him and he didn't look for me. I never met him even by chance. After all those years . . . I always thought that the future would lead him to me. I thought that all I had to do was to wait and he would come back.

Wait? I didn't wait. The parallel lines of my life met, crossed, and separated. The dykes gave way and the rush of water swept everything away, changed everything.

I didn't wait because I don't know how to wait.

I was confident that the Thinker would appear before me one day at a sudden turning, and he would say, like the first time: "It grabs me by the throat." He would ask me about my honey, as though he had left me the day before, and I would reply that he should look for the answer for himself; that it was up to him to stretch out his hand and put it between my thighs and taste. "The proof of the sweetness of the honey is the honey itself," says Ibn Arabi. I used to say it in front of him, and then he became the one who would repeat it, to teach me what I already knew.

The era After the Thinker begins now, while I am writing about him. I discover him only today, and I discover that this book is his book. As if he had sowed its seed in me, and I needed all these years for it to grow in me.

I remember how he used to say, "Write about those books that you love. You have to do it." I would laugh and reject the idea. I didn't dare even think about it. It has taken all these years, and a pretext, for me to find the courage to make a study of classic Arab books of erotica. To shout out loud what I was whispering in secret.

I needed all these years for the study to take me back to the time of the Thinker and give me the power to evoke him. So that I could make him public, too, so that he could become a story. The time of the Thinker.

Yesterday, the director came into my office. It was something serious, I felt it, the way he came in and closed the door behind him. I raised my head in a silent question.

"The director of the National Library called me. There is some news. For security reasons, the Americans have cancelled their participation in the Hell's Books exhibition and consequently the seminar in New York has been cancelled. The French said they couldn't bear the costs on their own. So we won't be going. What do you say? How far have you got with your presentation on the Arab books of erotica? Have you finished it? I'm so sorry. You can always publish it, and I'll help you with that. I am truly sorry."

Security reasons? A change of heart. I had been looking forward to seeing New York again, but never mind. What mattered was the book. And the Thinker I had created. I would publish the study: what need had I of the apologetic director, or the Americans and the French cowering in terror of the bogeyman of terrorism?

If they hadn't asked me to do it, I wouldn't have found the courage to write it, or to return to the time of the Thinker. Certainly, I must give them the credit for that, and thank them, simply, for their collaboration.

The Thinker was my secret, and the books were a part of that secret. Does the scandal lie in the deed, or in the revelation of the deed?

Who is asking the question?

My story is no scandal, nor is my book.

The scandal was in the secret.

But the secret is no longer.

Paris/Tunis
2005-2006

ABOUT THE AUTHOR

Salwa Al Neimi was born in Damascus,
Syria. Since the mid-seventies, she has
lived in Paris, where she studied Islamic
philosophy and theatre at the Sorbonne.
She has published five volumes of poetry
and a collection of short stories.